HIRED GUN

ALSO BY RYAN J. PELTON

Fiction

Dexter O'Kane Series

Stranger Danger (Book 2)

Color Blood (Book 3)

First Blood (Book 4)

L.A. Dreams (Book 5)

Dexter O'Kane Box Set (Books 1-4)

Stand Alone Titles

The Boardwalk

Corey Island (novella)

Watched (novella)

Young Adult

Running Down a Dream

Boonville (Boonville Series Book 1)

Middle Grade

Ricky Rayburn Series

Secrets of the Ambassadors (Book 1)

Mysterious Pirates of the Pacific (Book 2)

Non Fiction

The Modern Saints

Gospel Driven Leadership

The Gospel Marinated Soul

The Gospel Marinated Life

By Way of Reminder

Gospel Centered Productivity

Everyday Evangelism

40 Days with Jesus

HIRED GUN

A NOVEL

RYAN J. PELTON

Attention Books

To YOU the reader…
Thanks for taking a chance on me.
Thanks for the emails.
Thanks for the reviews.
Thanks for the support.
Thanks for following along…

Published by Attention Books
Attentionbooks.com

Paperback ISBN: 978-1-949420-04-3
Cover design by Attention Books
Edited by Kari Karandrakis

Printed in the United States of America
Fourth Edition: 2025

He has told you, O man, what is good;
and what does the Lord require of you
but to do justice, and to love kindness,
and to walk humbly with your God?
-Micah 6:8

CHAPTER ONE

DEATH AND RAIN MINGLED TOGETHER.

Drops of water bounced off a sea of black umbrellas that shot upward like skyscrapers. I shifted in my uncomfortable wooden chair, surrounded by hundreds of people listening to the pastor on the outdoor lawn.

A large, black casket, perched like a gargoyle, hovered over its eventual home: a silent hole waiting to embrace her victims.

Next to the larger one, a smaller box elbowed in—a size reserved for premature death. I looked up hard, trying to fight off tears.

The echoing of the pastor's voice was muted by small outbursts of weeping as the death boxes lowered into the ground. Outside, shells. Inside, souls. The hope of a merger in heaven.

I scratched my unshaven face, shifted to the side, and felt the wood stabbing my lower back. A five-o'clock-shadow was a reminder of two truths: I hate shaving most days, and when your family dies, it is not a high priority.

The flood of emotion choked my insides, hitting me like a truck plowing through a deer on the highway. I tried to breathe in normal time with little luck.

I bowed my head.

Tears dripped onto the grass, keeping time with the pounding rain.

My church shoes, reserved for Christmas, Easter, and an occasional funeral, were soaked with water and sadness.

Why, God? I breathed through the tears.

A large, warm arm wrapped around my slouching shoulders. "I'm sorry, brother. It's not right," John said, stroking the back of my black suit.

John Wood is my best friend. Partner in crime from life's first breath. The Wood and O'Kane families lived close together for most of their existence in LeClaire, Missouri. A small, blue-collar town, spattered with a few immigrants—my family included.

The O'Kane's emigrated from Ireland when my grandparents determined the lack of jobs would be a problem. They came to America in the 50's, looking for the American Dream. They found their slice of the pie in LeClaire.

My grandfather, a meat man—butcher, to be correct—operated a store on the corner of Main and Green. He worked hard, serving the people of LeClaire with beef, pork, and sausage. Many tables in our town were adorned with a sticker reading "The Local Pig".

I stared at my tear-stained hands and peered into John's bloodshot eyes. "Did I do something wrong? Why is this happening?" I said, leaning back in the wooden folding chair.

John's large hand swallowed mine. "Oh, man, don't even go there. You were a great husband and the best dad. Lisa and Spencer were fortunate to have you in their lives."

I loved Lisa more than life, like take-a-bullet, my-heart-hurts kind of love. The obsession originated at a high school basketball game. The LeClaire Bulldogs were playing our cross-town rival, the Greeley Gators. I didn't play basketball because uncoordinated Irish kids named Dexter didn't make the NBA. So I cheered from the stands.

Lisa danced across the gym floor, cheering on our school. She was the cheerleader and I the non-jock. Her long, blond hair bounced off her red and white skirt. I knew Lisa was the mythical One before she did.

We dated senior year and married the following summer. No reason to wait. Couples married young in small towns. In LeClaire, people view marriage and childbearing with different lenses compared to city folk. Having enough money or traveling to Europe before marriage is not considered in our town. Life begins and ends in LeClaire for her twenty thousand residents.

Spencer was born four years later. The happiest time of my life. A half-Irish, half-German grew and developed his own personality, and I hoped he would have more of the German side, and less of the too-much-drinking Irish side.

I promised a stable home to my family. My father left for prison when I was six. That's a story for another day.

The sounds of timpans, fifes, and bagpipes played *Be Thou My Vision*. A song played at our wedding. Nothing pierced deeper than authentic Irish folk music. When the bagpipes came out, it was celebration or death. No middle ground.

My father emigrated with his family from Ireland on his first birthday. He lived across the street from my mother and stalked her early. I wished he had used his tenacity for the common good.

I whispered in John's ear, "I need a drink. You want to head over to O'Malley's?"

John lurched forward as if being stung by a bee. "O'Kane, you can't leave. Can't a beer wait? Your family needs you, man."

My black tie pinched the life out of my thick Irish neck, and I gave it a tug. John peered at me, I gave a *let's get out of here* stare and nod. "I don't have a family; they're buried in the ground. O'Malley's for Happy Hour if you want a ride."

I slid out of the chair, used an umbrella to shield my identity, and moved like a cat burglar trying to escape the bagpipes, tears, and sadness. My head dropped and I tried not to make eye contact with any mourners as the rain intensified.

My tears stopped.

I walked through rows of gravestones, tapping them with my hand, counting the years between the lines.

Death is not fair.

From behind a tree a man appeared, wearing a black trench coat and holding an umbrella. I gave a half smile, and tried weaving to the left, and he stopped me in the center.

"Excuse me, pal. I'm just trying to get to the car," I said.

"This was no accident," the man said.

"What did you say?"

"These deaths were no accident," he said.

I pushed the man's right shoulder out of the way. "You don't know what you're talking about. I need to get to the car, psycho," I said.

He relented, and moved to the side.

I kept walking toward the car, rain falling, I looked back one more time.

The man disappeared behind a tree. I scanned the cemetery and browsed the green, wet landscape.

Gone.

I drank alone at O'Malley's.

CHAPTER
TWO

Six months later

"DEXTER, check out this lamp. I think we could score with this one," John said with a grin. He held up a vintage, green ceramic lamp, the pit stains under his arms in full view. "Bob, how much you want for this? I noticed a chip on the base. You need to consider that in the price." John pointed at the imperfection.

The art of *picking* is all about the Poker Face. You find a Pre-Civil War bowl, gun, or utensil in a barn in Duluth, Iowa. These small town folk have no idea the worth of the item. Most people we work with are trying to get rid of their "junk" and not concerned with making money. Mostly, it's kids or ex-wives unloading the picking of past family members. You keep excitement in check, smile, and low ball them. Celebrate later.

Occasionally, you will find the rare person who knows the market. I can spot it a mile away. They always want too much for their items. Not ready to let go of their junk. This is why you buy low and sell high. If not, move on.

I yelled across the barn to get John's attention, "Give him fifty for the lamp. Don't budge." He gave me a thumbs up in agreement.

My phone buzzed in my jean pocket. I struggled to get the phone out of my tight jeans, squinted to identify the number, and didn't recognize it.

"Hello, this is Antique Adventures, Dexter speaking."

A man with a deep voice began to speak. "Is this Dexter O'Kane?"

I looked over at John, making sure he wasn't screwing up the deal on the lamp. "Yes, this is Dexter."

"This call is being recorded for quality assurance. Please be advised," the mystery caller said in a formal tone.

I held my hand over the phone mouthpiece and motioned toward John. "I need to take this outside. Buy low and sell high," I mouthed. I turned my attention back to the phone. "I am here. What is this about?" I asked.

"My name is David and I am calling on behalf of American Express. I am calling in regards to the balance of your Gold Card. The card is currently over the credit limit and you are late on the last couple payments."

I felt my face get hot and stomach turn. I scratched my head and paced around the side of the large red barn. "How much is the balance?" I said with hesitation, knowing the ball park of the balance.

"You owe $50,000. If we do not receive at least a minimum payment in the next ten days we will need to take legal action and report you to the Credit Bureau. This will damage your credit."

When my wife and son passed, I did not have any money to pay for the medical bills and funeral. The only option was to put it all on credit cards. The antique-picking business has potential for money, but in the last six months it had been dry.

I spent too much time in sweatpants and sipping cheap beer at the local watering hole. All my fault.

I tried to use my picking-negotiating skills on Mr. American

Express. "So here's the deal. My wife and son died a few months ago. Do you have any kind of death-in-the-family grace period?"

There was a short pause on the other line, but he did not fall for it. "I am sorry to hear this, Mr. O'Kane. We do have a policy for those struggling to pay their bills."

For a moment, I felt God threw me a bone of grace. My face cooled and stomachache subsided.

"Thank you, sir. I am very grateful. What does this mean?" I asked.

"We will stop charging interest on the card for a full year and you only need to pay minimum payments. This will bring your payments down considerably. But, if you miss one payment at any point, the interest will turn back on, and you will be charged fees. Is this something you want to do, Mr. O'Kane?"

I banged my head against the barn and tapped the side of the phone, "That is all you can do? My wife died, for crying out loud!" I said with a mixture of anger and tears.

"Again, I am sorry for your loss, Mr. O'Kane. This is all we can do right now," the man said in a robotic tone.

I mulled it over in my head, knowing there were not many options at this point. "Okay, if that is all you can do. Sign me up."

"Please make your minimum payment in less than ten days and continue to do so for the next twelve months. You will be locked into the interest free rate. Anything else I can help you with today, Mr. O'Kane?"

I grinned from ear to ear. "Yes, pray I win the lottery, and if you can raise people from the dead, that would be great."

"I am sorry, Mr. O'Kane, we don't provide these services. Thank you for being an American Express customer."

The phone clicked dead.

I slid down the side of the barn and put my head down in shame. *I hope John makes money off the lamp or we are screwed.*

I limped back inside the barn and tried to pretend life was

okay. The hot face and stomachache returned as I thought about the phone conversation.

"How's it going, John? You get the lamp?"

He held up the green antique lamp like the Stanley Cup. "You bet, baby. Boom."

John lowered the lamp, placed a finger on my mouth, looked around the barn like he stole something, and began to whisper, "I totally got a steal. The lamp is worth at least 500 bucks. I low-balled him for $100." He laughed while his pudgy belly moved up and down. A circular, yellow sweat stain smiled back at me.

"Good work. Let's get out of here. I don't think there is much more to pick. This county is dry."

We jumped into the van and John turned to me, sipping a sixty-four-ounce Cherry Coke. "Who was on the phone? You looked stressed."

"Oh, nothing. It was a sales call trying to get me to buy stationary for the shop."

The van hurled down the quiet highway of Missouri.

I stared out the window, thinking about my family, the phone call, and if I was going to make it. The pressure of debt and lying to my best friend added to the hurting stomach."

"John, could you run through the next drive-thru? I need 7-UP; my stomach is on fire."

"You got it. I need to refill my Cherry Coke anyway," John said, sipping the last drop of his bucket of sugar water.

I pulled the curtains back between the passenger seats and the back storage space of the van and peered in. At least the green lamp looked nice.

CHAPTER
THREE

I SIPPED my 7-UP as we made our way down the highway, back to the shop in LeClaire, Missouri. My stomach began to settle.

The stomach pain was an everyday routine dealing with the death of my family, failing business, and did I mention, new drug habit.

I try to ease my conscience by telling myself… *at least my drug of choice is not the hard stuff. It's just marijuana.* Old ladies with cancer smoke it for medicinal purposes. Why not me?

John peered over at me, eyes hovering above his giant bucket of Cherry Coke. "How's the stomach? Seems like you're getting stomach pain a lot lately. Maybe you should have that checked out?"

I am not one for doctors these days. The last extended stay in the hospital was watching my wife and son be taken off machines to keep them alive.

I would consider a prescription for medical marijuana. But, a visit to the doctors for a stomachache is not high priority these days. Besides, more money to pay.

"I'll be fine. I'm just a little stressed these days," I said, hoping the small talk would end.

John continued to slurp his drink and he inquired, "I know this is awkward. I am not sure how to ask this. How are you dealing with the death of Lisa and Spencer? Are you seeing a counselor? Getting help?"

John was a good friend, but did not know how to enter into another person's pain, like most men. He avoided any kind of conversation related to the tough stuff of life. Kansas City Chiefs football. Missouri State anything. No problem.

He prefers life fun and light.

"I'll be fine. I don't need to spend money on a counselor who is going to give me back rubs and tell me everything is going to be fine by positive thinking," I said, staring out the window at the flat Missouri landscape.

John threw his hands in the air. "No problem. Just know I am in your corner."

John turned on the radio and cranked up the volume. "No sense sitting in silence. Let's rock"—putting up devil horns with his fingers.

I began to nod off in the passenger seat of our Volvo extended van, Led Zeppelin fading in and out of my ears, my phone ringing in my pocket.

I fiddled in my pocket, searching for the phone. I tried to gain composure. I held it up and squinted at the screen.

"Shit. It's Maria."

A loud and bubbly Spanish accent blasted through my ear drums, "Dexter, it's Maria. How did the pick go? You better have gotten me something good."

Maria Gonzalez was our store manager in LeClaire. A total find. She came to Antique Adventures a few years ago when the business was booming. We needed help sustaining sales and pick leads. She found the best picking spots in the country.

She was a single mom. Three kids. A jerk ex-husband who abused her, ran away with another woman, and doesn't send child support. Maria had a temper, but she was a good saleswoman, knew small towns, and understood small town people. A perfect fit for us.

I paused for a second, looked over at John, and then back at the road. "Umm… yeah, we did alright. John picked up a vintage lamp. Should make us a few hundred bucks."

Maria shot back in a loud voice, "A few hundred bucks? You silly white boys. The money supply is low. You need to stay out and do some freestyling."

Freestyling is my favorite kind of picking. You drive through small towns and the backroads of America to find rusty gold. Barns. Storage sheds. Abandoned cars. All signs of possible monetary gain.

We walk up to the door, explain we are "pickers", and ask if we can look around. You might be threatened or invited to look around. All depends on how smooth the approach.

I love the rush of freestyling. It reminds me why I got into the business. It brings back the childlike awe of finding treasure and searching worlds unknown. I'm a romantic picker.

"I don't want to freestyle today. We are exhausted and coming home. I know the cash is low, but we can get out there tomorrow and make a score."

I imagined Maria waving her freshly-painted long fingernails and pointing them at the phone. "No way, Señor. You get out on the road. Find something to sell. I got babies to feed."

I smiled at John. This was everyday Maria. We both knew. "Don't worry, my Mexican princess. I picked up that 1921 Indian motorcycle last week. I have a guy who wants it. We can get a few thousand out of it. I will call him tomorrow," I said, hoping to calm Maria down.

"Okay, Señor Dexter. You sell the motorcycle tomorrow, or plan on freestyling in the afternoon," Maria shot back.

Maria hung up the phone and the only sound we heard were tires on a quiet highway. I mumbled under my breath, "We are screwed. I need to win the lottery or my picking days are over."

The idea of smoking a joint brought a smile to my face.

CHAPTER
FOUR

THE PORCH FILLED with marijuana smoke, wafting up to the heavens like an offering to the gods. I leaned back and forth on my white rocking chair wondering how I got here. Literally here. And here, here. An emotional rawness opened with each puff of smoke.

The effects of smoking pot set in. Calmness. Each expanding lung creating peace.

A second effect. Lightness of the head. A third. Blurry eyes. All the effects made life manageable for the moment.

I gazed out from the porch to my large piece of Missourian land in the country. My stepfather's motto was, *real men have land.* So that is what I did.

Fall in full swing, changing leaves and colors, cool breezes, and bearable weather. My dog Murphy slept sideways on the porch, without a care in the world.

Puff. Puff. Deep inhale. Freedom. The more I smoked, the more my mind went back. Back to when my family was alive.

My eyes began to flutter, daydreaming about Lisa calling from the house, giving the countdown until dinner. The smell of soup and fresh bread swimming through our nostrils. Spencer and I throwing the football in the front yard as Murphy jumped on our clothes, trying to steal the ball.

With another puff my memory, the lines of the present and past began to blur. Not sure if I was alive, dead, or dreaming. A ringing sound echoed in the background.

I saw Lisa in an apron, answering the phone in her sweet Missourian accent. Calling out to pick up the phone. *Honey, it's your dad. Don't talk too long. Dinner is almost ready.*

The dream state vanished in a puff of marijuana smoke and the present hell came back into view. My phone rang, startling me from almost-sleep. I sat motionless and blurry eyed as my joint slowly burned down, almost burning my fingers. I threw it across the porch, onto the ground.

John was calling.

Ignored.

The voicemail alert popped up on the screen. I held the phone for a second, contemplating a call back. I looked around the yard again.

I slid my thumb across the screen to get into the voicemail mode. I propped the phone up to my ear and pretended to be interested. The pot high continued to affect my focus and brain function.

John ranted and yelled on the other line, "Dexter. I just talked to Maria at the shop. She showed me the books. We need to talk." I mocked John by mouthing what he just said on the phone.

Blah. Blah. Blah.

Sooner or later, John would find out. The reality of my deep debt could only be hidden for so long. The combination of a dead family, poor business decisions, and a budding drug habit would be my nemesis.

I did not care anymore.

At the moment, my head clear and free, nothing mattered right now.

Effect number four. Hunger. What we call the munchies.

Usually involving copious amounts of pizza and Doritos. My stomach growled back at me.

I reached down and stroked Murphy. I wondered if sitting on the porch, forever, might be my escape plan. Maybe ignoring John, Maria, business, and life would be the new plan. Not to mention creditors, banks, and many annoying customers in LeClaire.

God took away the only thing I cherished more than life itself. My family.

Something had to give. Right?

The buzz of the weed began to subside. I picked up my phone and stared at the numbers.

I need to call John back. I gotta call him. He's my best friend. Buddies can't be liars. Bro code. But, first, I need to get something to eat. Munchies, bad.

After a couple minutes, I came back to the porch with a plate of cold pizza, Doritos, and a frothy beer.

I made the call. "Hey, John. I got your call."

"When were you going to tell me? It's bad, Dexter... real bad," John said, trailing off.

"I know, man. I'm sorry I didn't tell you. With my family thing, I was embarrassed, and tried to fix it on my own."

"I don't pretend to understand what you are going through. But, we need to get this fixed or we are going out of business."

I picked up a piece of pepperoni pizza and tried to talk and chew at the same time. "I know. I will be in this afternoon. We can do a local freestyle and get something going," I said, slurping my beer.

John agreed and hung up the phone. I set the phone on a small side table and continued to devour the pizza and chips without hesitation. The munchies were in full force.

I took another sip of my beer and continued to stare into the yard, daydreaming about when life was normal. Lisa was spinning Spencer around by the arms as they laughed and giggled in the cool fall air.

For a moment it felt real.

I leaned back in my rocker and gently rocked to the rhythm of the breeze blowing through the yard. My eyes began to flutter in and out of consciousness.

Finally they gave in, and I nodded off to sleep. The dog snored with me.

Effect number five: blackouts.

CHAPTER
FIVE

THE DIESEL FORD F-150 rumbled into the Antique Adventures parking lot. A gravel drive led up to a large, square, steel warehouse with a glass door entry leading into the store. Old cars, signs, and a smattering of antique motorcycles were propped up in the well-manicured, landscaped yard for interested buyers.

Antique Adventures was my dream job. I grew up in small town Missouri, which encouraged imagination. When there is not a lot to do, finding old bicycles and turning them into pirate ships is required. Old cans become dangerous weapons used for the hunt.

From a young age, I knew how to find and sell my rusty gold. If there was a job where imagination, adventure, and commerce could come together, that would be the dream. It beats working in the lumber yard like most of my friends. Most days, I was amazed that this is how I paid the bills.

Today was not one of those days.

Like a dog with his tail between his legs, I slowly walked into the shop, grabbing the large, glass doors and swinging them open. My dog Murphy followed on my heels.

An awkward silence greeted me as John and Maria stood behind the counter, pretending not to see me.

I played the game. "Hey, guys. How are things? I noticed the Indian motorcycle is still in the yard. No luck?"

Maria tapped her long, red fingernails on the counter, snapping her gum. "Why didn't you tell us?" Her face turned sad rather than angry. "We are not mad... more disappointed. You talk about being family. You're not acting like one with the lying."

I adjusted a lampshade, an item on our last pick. I tried not to stare them directly in the eye. "I know. I was wrong. I got embarrassed and did not know what to do after my wife died. I was a mess."

John walked out from behind the counter and put an arm around me. "Dude. How many years have we been friends?"

"Our entire lives."

"You can tell us anything. We know you are in a tough spot and still healing. Let's just try to be honest. We are family."

The dog nudged against my leg. I reached down to pet his ears. "Stupid, I know. I tried to get us some business by hiring an advertising agency. It cost a fortune and did not result in many sales."

Maria raised her hand. "Dexter, you know advertising never works. We are a word-of-mouth business. We are old school. We hit the pavement and make money the old fashioned away, one person at a time, one pick at a time."

John gave another family speech: "We are a family and need to run big decisions by one another. No more secrets."

"You got it," I said in agreement. I felt a tear in my eye, thinking about how much John and Maria became family after Lisa and Spencer.

John and Maria looked at each other. "Maria and I talked while you were gone. We need to go on a big run and get things back in order. She found a guy about fifty miles away that has a boatload of stuff for us to look through. We are going to get back in the black, one pick at a time. We're heading out now."

Maria held out her arms covered in a leopard print shirt. "We need to hug." We hugged it out, and John and I left the shop. The job felt like a dream again. A little dream.

CHAPTER
SIX

A RENEWED sense of hope and energy pulsated through my bones. We drove down Highway 17 in the Volvo, headed fifty miles south to New Haven for a possible pick. We arrived at a long-winding gravel road taking us to the house.

"I think this is it," John said, looking down to confirm on his GPS. On each side of the gravel road were sheds, barns, warehouses, old cars, signs, and piles of rusted debris.

My eyes widened. A glimpse of picker heaven. The more rusted-out junk, the better chance to find the big score.

I rubbed a rabbit's foot hanging from the rearview mirror. "Your turn," I said. I nodded at John.

The rabbit foot was a souvenir from my only hunting trip with Spencer. We needed this pick to be a good one or we might be walking the unemployment line.

John and I walked up to the ranch-style house. We were greeted by a nicely-trimmed yard and a plethora of small ceramic gnomes placed in a variety of scenes.

We gave a couple knocks on the door, and a frail man with a white beard and missing teeth greeted us with a smile.

"Howdy. Are you the guys Maria told me were coming?" he asked, sticking out a deformed hand.

I greeted him, "We sure are. Here's a flyer that gives a list of things we are looking for."

The bearded man gazed down at the paper and pushed his glasses up to get a better view. "By the way, my name is Frank Ford." He pointed at the items on the list. "I got almost everything on the list. Let's go to my barn in the back and get started."

We walked around the side of the brown house and a large, blue barn came into view. Two large, white wooden doors were in the front. From the size of the barn, it was filled to the brim with junk. The perfect place to get us back on track. My heart thumped with possibility.

"I've been collecting for forty years. I got hooked after college, when I started collecting vinyl records. I started small and now I have barns full," he said, unlocking a chain on the barn door.

John and I walked through the barn eyes wide open, scanning shelves, and pointing at items like kids in a toy shop. The rusty gold climbed from floor to ceiling. The kind of break we were hoping for.

John looked over at me, smiled, and elbowed me in the side. "Where do we begin?"

There is a strategy to picking. When you walk into a situation, like a giant barn filled with rusty gold, it can be overwhelming. Don't panic.

You pick a side of the barn and work your way to the middle. This ensures you don't miss or overlook the next big score. It can't be a leisurely stroll. You need to climb in the junk, touching, scouring, and exploring all the contents. The best gold often hides under other gold.

I took charge. "John, you start on the left, I will start on the right, and we can work to the middle."

Our eyes darted up and down the walls of junk like staring at art in a museum. These rusty relics were our Mona Lisa, Monet, and Michelangelo.

Clocks, vases, signs, and old tools hung off rusted metal hooks and shelves. I pulled a shopping cart out of the rubble.

I waved Frank over.

"Can I use this shopping cart for our finds?" I dusted off some mud from the handle.

"No problem. Fill that baby up. The fuller it gets, the more money I make," he said with a hearty laugh.

A woman's voice echoed from outside the barn doors.

"I think my wife is calling me. I'll be right back." Frank left the barn and disappeared out of sight.

We continued our pick. Climbing, digging, and examining all the items of history gone by. Old bikes, books, and lamps telling stories of days of yesteryear.

A faint scream perked my ears. I looked over at John, who was examining an old railroad tie. "You hear that?"

"What? My stomach has been rumbling for the last hour. I am starving," John said, rubbing his inflated stomach.

"No. I thought I heard a woman scream." I put my head down and continued to dig through a mound of old car parts. I heard the scream a second time. "I know you heard that."

We stopped picking and sauntered over to the front entrance of the barn. I looked both ways, trying to find the screaming person.

An older man with tattered clothing had Frank wrapped up from behind, a knife held to his neck and shouting intelligible words.

"You think you can betray me and get away with it?" the mystery attacker spewed with a red face.

Frank slumped in the arms of the attacker, pleading with him. "Please don't do this. This is a misunderstanding. We can make it right. I have a family."

We knelt down behind a rusted-out Oldsmobile, trying not to be in sight of the attacker. The wife screamed and pleaded. "Please don't hurt him. Let him go; he has done nothing to you."

The armed man spun Frank around to get a better look at the wife. "What do you know? You are just as guilty."

"Please, we can pay you. Take anything you want."

The argument ceased and a moment of silence hushed across the yard. We peered around the front of the car, our hearts beating in our mouths, and shirts sweaty with fear.

"The payment I need is not monetary. It needs to be with blood."

With a quick flick of the wrist, the knife slit Frank's throat and he bled out like a stuck pig. Blood spewed all over the ground as he crumbled to the ground.

Dead in an instant. Making no sound.

The wife huddled over the dead body, weeping, her tears falling into the pools of blood and mud on the ground.

John and I ran out from behind the cars to try and get a better glimpse at the killer. He disappeared around the house and vanished.

CHAPTER
SEVEN

JOHN BENT down over the widow and consoled her. I fumbled with my phone, trying to get ahold of LeClaire PD. Difficult in a small town. My heart raced as I replayed the murder in my head. The screams of a woman watching her husband bleed out played in my ear like a broken record.

The phone connected. "Yes, this is Dexter O'Kane. I need to report a murder."

The dispatcher calmly asked for a location. I scanned the yard, looking for an identifier.

"We're off Highway 17. I don't know the address. I'm from out of town. Hold on a second…"

I ran to the front of the house, cell phone shaking in my hand. A set of silver numbers gleamed from the sunlight on a duck-shaped mailbox. "The address is 4011 Oak Road."

The dispatcher perked up with confidence. "Are you at the Ford residence?"

Another reminder of small-town living, as everyone knows everyone. "Please come quickly; the victim is not breathing."

I hung up the phone, and rushed back to the barn where John, Mrs. Ford, and Mr. Ford were, the last not moving, his neck wide open, blood pooling up on the ground.

Mrs. Ford sat silently over her dead husband. Sobs turned to whimpers.

"I called the police. They should be here soon."

John rubbed the back of Mrs. Ford and stumbled on words. "It-It's going to be okay. An ambulance will be here soon. I'm so sorry."

A few minutes later, a police car and ambulance pulled into the gravel driveway. Two men jumped out of the vehicle with a look of concern. One officer was tall and lanky, while the other needed to push back from the table more often.

The donut-lover spoke up first. "I'm Officer Smithville and this is Officer Stiles. We had a report of an assault?" His voice cracked like a teenager in puberty.

I shook my head. "He's gone." I greeted the officers and pointed toward John and Mrs. Ford sitting on the ground. "Right over here, officers."

The lanky officer spoke into his shoulder, "This is dispatch 301. We are going to need a coroner to 4011 Oak Road, off Highway 17. Please come quickly, possible homicide." The walkie talkie squelched off as he examined the scene.

Mrs. Ford, in her tear-filled turmoil, and John, trying to console her, forced the officers to speak to me. "Can you tell us what happened?"

I placed a hand on my forehead and tried to retell the last minutes to the officers. "To be honest, I am not sure. My friend and I, John, came out here to do a pick—"

The fat cop butted in. "Pick?"

"Yes, we are pickers. We go around and look for antiques and other junk to sell in our store."

"Oh."

"We were in the blue barn behind us and were looking around. We heard Mrs. Ford screaming outside. We came out of the barn and saw a man with Mr. Ford in a headlock with a knife on his neck."

The officer held a small notepad and scribbled furiously as the skinny cop interrogated. "Did you see what he looked like?"

"We were hiding behind that rusted-out Oldsmobile and could not get a clear look from this distance. Although, I did notice a white beard and he was tall. Maybe six feet"—I pointed to the skinny officer—"about your height and build."

The fat officer cleared his throat. "I used to be his size before I discovered donuts."

I shot back, "You don't say?"

As we continued to talk an ambulance pulled up in the background. Two people jumped out of the vehicle, a man and woman. The cops pointed to Mr. Ford's body. They asked John and Mrs. Ford to stand back as they checked his vitals.

No signs of life.

"The coroner and detectives will need to finish up here. They will be here shortly," the officer said.

John wrapped his arms around Mrs. Ford as she stared at her dead husband. She covered her face.

The officers thanked me for the time and moved on to Mrs. Ford. "Ma'am, do you mind if we ask you a couple questions?"

The wife tried to pull herself together as she wiped tears and snot from her nose.

"Did you get a good look at the man who attacked your husband? Would there be any reason for him to do so?"

Mrs. Ford suddenly got calm and then animated. "Of course I saw him. I think he's my husband's uncle, I've seen him in pictures. His name is Jack; people call him Hobo Jack."

Now scribbling at a frantic pace and smiling a half smile, the skinny cop grew excited. "Why might he want to hurt your husband?"

Mrs. Ford held her hands akimbo on her hips. "I have no idea. No one in the family has seen him for years. We didn't even think he was alive." The officers nodded and scribbled. "He showed up to the house, unannounced. The next thing I know, he is slicing my husband open."

Tears began to well up again in her eyes as she stared down at the dirt floor.

The officers glanced over at the paramedics to determine their pace. "Looks like they're done," said the fat one. "Why don't you head with them to the morgue? I will need to speak with you at the station for more questioning at some point. I know right now is not a good time."

The ambulance lights lit up with no siren. It sped off down the highway, gravel kicking off its tires. The police cruiser did the same.

John and I stood in the middle of the gravel driveway, silent. I peeked at the pooled-up blood, now a soupy, muddy mixture. I looked at John.

"Are you shitting me right now? Did that just happen?"

"Only in small-town America," John said, shaking his head and giving a toothy grin.

We hopped back into the van and sped off down the highway with no picks to show for. Only a dead body.

Maria was going to be pissed.

CHAPTER
EIGHT

TWO HOURS LATER, the only sounds in the van were bald tires churning south on Highway 17. I couldn't erase the movie playing in my head of witnessing my first murder. The only comparable thing being *Law and Order* reruns shown every five minutes on cable.

Murders were front page news in every big city in America. Not common in barns located in rural America. My years of picking with John brought us into interesting situations. Like when a barn caught fire after the owner dropped a cigarette in a can of gasoline. Watching the murder of a man in cold blood is not my idea of normal.

I spoke first. "What are we going to tell Maria? She is going to kill us if we come home empty-handed. Should we freestyle before we get back to the shop? I know a spot a few exits down."

"Come on, Dex. Maria might be full of angry Mexican blood and ready to snap, but I think she'll give us a break after witnessing a murder," John said.

There are two things Maria gets fired up over: When she arranges a pick and the people don't show up, and when we come home empty-handed.

John and I did a pick in Ohio and came home with only an

old Texaco gas sign. We made $50. I thought she was going to call up one of her Mexican drug cartel uncles and have us surface in the Ohio River.

"Okay, who's going to call her?" I asked, gritting my teeth.

"Let's rock-paper-scissor for it." John clenched a fist and placed inside the other.

"1-2-3 go. 1-2-3 go. 1-2-3 go."

In a best of five, John lost.

John pleaded for pardon. "I just consoled a lady whose husband got shivved in the neck. You know, that takes a lot out of me, with the emotional stuff. I can't deal with Maria right now."

I gave John a "you owe me" look. "I'll call."

I picked up my cell phone and stared down John. "Maria, this is Dexter. I got bad news."

An image of a red-faced Maria with steam blowing from her ears flashed in my mind. I waited for an attack.

"Come again, white boy. You better have something for me."

"We showed up for the pick. A great spot, by the way. And… the craziest thing happened."

Maria sighed. "Don't tell me you didn't get nothing."

I hesitated, adjusted my John Deere hat, and tried to pick my next words carefully. "Um, well, not exactly. We did not get much. But we saw something."

"You better have seen Jesus on the side of a barn or I don't care."

"We saw a murder."

Maria gave a kind of half laugh confused remark, "Is this one of your little white boy jokes? I don't have time for this. We need money. I have babies to feed."

"Not a joke. John and I were picking and a guy got his throat slit. We saw the whole thing."

"Are you okay?" Maria asked.

"Yeah. We're fine. The man bleeding out like a stuck pig is not fine. We're heading home."

"*Ay caramba*! I don't know what to say. Sorry about the white boy jokes."

"Thanks, Maria."

I hung up the phone and stared at the glowing pink sun setting in the distance. The craving for a hit of weed spurred on from the endless green fields of Missouri farmland.

I didn't want John to know about the new habit. Especially since I was spending company money to fuel the addiction. All in due time.

"How did Maria take it?" John asked.

"She's cool. It's all good," I said, picturing myself walking in the fields, lighting up the tall strands of grass, and smoking it.

"Pretty crazy day, huh? Probably didn't think you'd witness a murder when you rolled out of bed in your flannel pajamas," John said with a laugh.

"I'd like to roll something," I said under my breath.

"What's that?"

"Nothing."

I tried to fight off the urge to laugh and light one up. I got serious. "John, what are you feeling right now?"

"About what?"

"The murder."

John mulled it over for a moment. "I feel relieved. Glad we're safe. Kinda pissed the murderer ruined our pick. You?"

I looked out the window. The sun only a sliver disappearing behind a small hill. "I want to do something about it."

"Do something about it? Like what? The cops came, ambulance came—what are you going to do?" John asked.

"I don't know. Ever since Lisa and Spencer died, there's been a gnawing in my gut. Like I need to make things right. Like I've been wronged by the universe. Like something or someone needs payback. When I saw Ford get killed, something broke."

John reached out and patted me on the arm. "These feelings are probably normal. You've seen three deaths in the last few months and that's a lot to handle. Let's get some space from this and you'll be fine."

"You're probably right. What am I going to do, anyway? Things happen for a reason. I don't really understand it all the time... but shit happens," I said.

John put his hand up for a high five. "Let's get back to the shop, figure out our next pick, and try to forget about today. You want a Cherry Coke? My treat."

"Sounds good," I said, still thinking about the joint. And, justice.

CHAPTER NINE

THE AIR-CONDITIONING UNIT kicked on at the offices of Antique Adventures, making goose bumps on my arms. My black leather swivel chair squeaked in the sterile room. I held a framed picture of Lisa and Spencer, occasionally touching it like they were alive.

I set the frame down, put my boots on the desk, and examined a handful of Excel spreadsheets. The quarter didn't look promising if we didn't score soon. I prayed the 1921 Indian motorcycle sold soon, or we would be searching for work.

Antique Adventures started as a hobby. My love for collecting rusty gold dated back to scouring the alleys, neighborhood trash cans, and dumpsters at the supermarket in LeClaire. The junk in question attaches to a story. A story of people, events, and experiences.

On the backroads of America, your story intersects with theirs. The rusty item connects to hopes, dreams, and the loss of loved ones. One man's junk, another man's treasure. One man's junk, another person's dead husband. Junk equals life. This one-time hobby was now a lucrative business supporting multiple employees. And hopes of a new store in another city. Let me not get ahead of myself.

I stared at the computer screen filled with numbers bringing a knot into my stomach. *Would it be easier to shut down the shop … no. I won't go down without a fight. This is not only my livelihood, it involves John and Maria too…*

A knock on the door shook me from my pity party. "Come in," I said, setting my feet on the floor.

John rushed into my office, waving a newspaper around like a man had just walked on the moon. He slammed it on my desk.

"Dex. Guess who made the morning paper?"

I hovered over the paper and read the headline story. "What did you expect? Nothing happens in small towns. When a murder happens, everyone is going to know."

John poked at the paper, almost knocking it off the desk. "Dude, read right here." I scanned the story, mouthing the words as I read, looking up slowly at John. His face grew calm.

"You don't think?"

"Oh, I do think. The guy who killed Ford is the same guy who killed later that day. It has to be," John said, smiling and crossing his arms in satisfaction.

The paper in my hand, I leaned back in the swivel chair, trying to comprehend the article. "The murderer comes to Ford's place and slits his throat. Up the road, another guy is killed in the same way, a few hours later. Sounds related to me. I'm no investigator … but this is a no-brainer. Right?"

The story did not give any hints of who was committing the crimes and did not have many leads. John ripped the paper back out of my hands. "Glad we got out of there yesterday in one piece. This guy seems like a psycho on a rampage."

"How does this happen? A guy goes around killing people and vanishes into thin air. No leads. I know we live in a small town, but everyone knows everyone."

A surge of rage bubbled up in my gut. I slammed my hand on the table. "This guy needs to be stopped."

John put his hands on his hips and pretended to take a step

back, mocking me. "What are you going to do, tough guy? You are an antique collector. Let the professionals handle this one."

I didn't like the way my wife and son's accident was handled. The community of LeClaire was still reeling from their deaths. What appeared to be an accident never sat well with me.

Now, with two murders in a neighboring community, I was not poised to handle this. Nor was LeClaire. "This is too much, John! Our community does not need to go through this again. We don't deserve this."

John leaned in and tried to calm me from my irrational tirades. He smiled and then turned serious. "Like I said … I am not sure what we're supposed to do. This is out of our league, old friend. We can support the police and our community. Other than that, I am not sure how we can help."

I leaned back in the swivel chair, hands behind my head. "I know. I don't know what I was thinking. I'm just tired of life right now. It seems all chaos and no peace," I said, staring at the ceiling.

"You know what helps the blues?" John asked.

"What?" I didn't want to say *weed*.

"Poker. Come over to my place tonight at seven. Beersley, Rollins, and Sawyer are coming over. Drown your sorrows in a couple beers and we will happily take all your money," John said, grinning.

Poker night was a tradition for the last ten years. I hadn't been in months. The thought of losing more money did not sound all that appetizing.

CHAPTER
TEN

AT 7 PM, Led Zeppelin played *Stairway to Heaven* through the bar jukebox. Voices chirped with laughter and banter unfamiliar to my recent isolation. When you are a walking contradiction, avoiding social interaction is easy.

Between the new drug habit, burying my family in the ground, and the fast-approaching reality of a tanking business, avoidance was warranted. At least, that was what I told myself, and what I told John when I bailed on Poker night.

I waved over the bartender. "Can I get a Jack and Diet Coke?"

A cloud of smoke hovered over the shelves of booze and boozers. Zeppelin murmured in the background. Only in small towns can you still smoke in bars. People in LeClaire are not sophisticated like those in New York, Los Angeles, and Kansas City. We don't obsess over organic foods and what might cause cancer. We work hard and drink hard—in no particular order.

I nodded at the petite, brown-haired bartender, as she nestled my drink on a napkin and dropped a short, red straw into its dark liquid.

O'Malley's is the only quasi-Irish pub in LeClaire. The next-closest one being in Kansas City, over two hundred miles away.

Bob Barker, the owner, is not Irish. He visited Ireland with his wife twenty years ago for their ten-year anniversary. He was never the same. He loved the culture and always dreamed about opening a pub. You might even catch him speaking with an Irish accent with enough drinks in him.

I am half-blooded Irish. The other half is German, thanks to my mother's gene pool. My mother was born in Germany and moved to the states with her family in the fifties, like many immigrants in LeClaire.

She ended up in small-town Missouri because her father was a farmer in Germany. He was able to run his own farm, living off the land, on the outskirts of LeClaire. Living the American Dream with his growing family. The hope of every immigrant.

The pub is not exactly purebred Irish. A mixture of bagpipes, dark beers, Irish nachos, deer heads and juke boxes. Not exactly what you would find in the homeland.

I nursed my Jack and Diet Coke, twirling the straw around in concentric circles, imagining my life as a continual swirl of chaos.

The door opened and a momentary flash of light shot through the darkened pub catching the corner of my eye. A tall, blonde woman emerged. My eyes locked on her for a moment and turned away, trying not to be that guy. My heart skipped a beat, thinking Lisa had just walked in to greet me for a drink. Their similarities were uncanny.

The mystery blonde sat a couple of high-top chairs away from me. She ordered a chardonnay and picked at the pretzels sitting in a bowl next to her. I tried to be inconspicuous by peeking around the bar at the twenty or so patrons, only giving an occasional uninterested stare.

I sipped my drink until the empty slurping sounds of "give me another" alerted my buzzed body. I stood up, placed a ten on the bar top, and glanced down to the woman. I was lonely, and a little friendly conversation with a woman other than Maria would be good for me.

I picked up my drink and set it next to her. "I don't usually do this. I saw you come in and wanted to say hello. My name is Dexter O'Kane, and I'm lonely."

The woman faked a smile with mascara lines painted down her face.

Startled at the woman's face, I said, "I'm sorry. It's obvious you are going through something"—I pointed back to my seat—"so I am going to go back over there and leave you alone."

The mystery woman reached out her red, manicured nails and placed her hand gently on mine. "Stay. I could use the company. Dexter, was it?"

The soft touch of her hand sent tingles shooting through my body. It had been six months since I held Lisa. The woman brought strong memories of her back to mind. I tried to fight back the tears.

"So what brings you to O'Malley's?" I asked. "The deer heads or Irish nachos? I have not seen you in here before."

She tapped her nails on the bar. "Where do I begin? For starters, I don't usually go to bars. My conservative Catholic upbringing doesn't allow for these kinds of establishments. But, today has been shit, I need a drink, and my priest can hear it from me later at confession."

I nodded, enjoying her honesty and the tone of her voice. I swirled the ice cubes around in my drink, trying to think of a line. This was new to me, having the same woman for the last fifteen years. "Why is today shit? I bet it's no worse than mine."

"Oh, really?" she said with a competitive tone. "Does your bad day involve murder?"

I pushed my drink aside and grabbed a pretzel from the communal bowl. "Actually, it does. I was a witness to a murder yesterday. You?"

Taking a sip of her chardonnay and rolling her eyes, she answered, "I don't believe you. The chances of two people coming into a bar and both being connected to a murder in a tiny town like LeClaire. Not possible. Is this a line?"

I laughed and chewed on a piece of ice. "I have not used a line since high school. Go ahead. Tell me your story. Nothing surprises me these days."

She grabbed a napkin to wipe the mascara streaks from her eyes and took another swig of wine. "A family member of mine was murdered yesterday. I don't know all the details and I am not sure who the killer is. Our family thinks it might be a distant relative."

I let the words sink in for a moment. "Wow. That's not what I expected. It seems a lot of people are getting killed near LeClaire as of late."

She shook her head. Locks of blonde hair passed in front of her blue eyes like windshield wipers in a rainstorm. "Can we start over? I didn't even introduce myself. My name is Samantha Rose." She reached out her red fingernails and skinny wrists.

"I'm Dexter. My friends call me Dex."

"I know. You're the lonely guy with no lines."

"Well, good. We are no longer strangers and now can share our sad stories with one another." We lifted our glasses for a cheers.

I lied through my teeth, "I usually don't come to these places either. Only on really bad days. I am glad we met."

Noticing that both of our glasses were empty, I waved to the bartender. "One more Jack and Diet Coke, and whatever she's drinking."

"That is very sweet of you. I usually don't let first dates buy," she said, smiling.

"Think of it as a gift to forget about a really crappy day," I said.

We clinked our glasses and I talked with Samantha for the rest of the night. It felt good to be social again.

CHAPTER
ELEVEN

MORNING SUNLIGHT POKED through the curtains, jolting my eyes open. I lay in the bed, trying to jog a sluggish brain from a night of drinking. The familiar brown paint and neon alarm clock alerted me to home.

Each throb of a headache matched the amounts of drinks consumed. In a moment of panic, I shot up from the bed, sheets flailing to the floor. *Oh crap, the girl at the bar.*

I ran into the living room and stopped at the couch. The cushions were covered with a mix of pillows, sheets, and blankets. A note sat in the center of the coffee table.

Dex, thanks for the drinks, conversation, and letting me crash on the couch last night. You were a true gentlemen. I am sorry I left in a hurry. Needed to work a morning shift at the hospital. Call me. 555-909-5463. Samantha.

I held up the note and tried to recall the night—without much luck. *Man, I am glad I didn't do anything I would regret.*

I went into the kitchen to make a large pot of coffee. I sipped coffee on the porch, petted my dog Murphy, and began to recall conversation with Samantha. A story about throwing her brother in the Missouri River while on vacation.

The best.

It made me smile.

The theme of murder kept coming up in the reservoir of my mind. The chances of two murders happening on the same day in a small town like LeClaire.

Strange at best.

I called John.

"You got a minute?"

"We missed you last night. Thanks for bailing on us, pal," John said.

"Sorry. I didn't feel social last night. But, I did meet a woman at O'Malley's."

John shot back, "I thought you weren't in the mood to be social."

"Nothing happened. We had a couple drinks and that was it."

"You've been a lonely guy lately. You sure that's all that happened?" John said, giggling on the other line.

I held the phone away from my face and mouthed the words *I hate you*. "Anyway ... when we talked, she mentioned someone in her family getting murdered a couple days ago. I'm not sure the connection. You think this could be connected to the Ford murder?"

"Dex, we already talked about this. You don't need to be LeClaire's private investigator. Competent people are working on the case. It's probably just a coincidence," John said.

I shot back, "A coincidence? A woman comes into a bar in a town of less than twenty thousand. Talks about a family member being murdered. Coincidence? I think not."

"Even if they are connected, I am not sure what you want to do. You need to get your crap together. This is not the time to play private eye," John said.

"I know. I can't seem to get these murders out of my head. Something has to be done. People are not going to get killed in my town and have their killers run free," I said, pacing on the front porch.

"You know what you need?" John asked.

"A beer?"

"No. It's only eight o'clock. You need to go picking."

I knew going on a pick was needed to stop the bleeding of the business. There were only a couple things in life that made me happier. Finding rusty gold was tops on the list.

"Freestyle?" I asked.

"Of course. You can be a private investigator some other time. Let's do what you were born to do," John said.

I hung up the phone and sipped on my now-cold coffee. I looked out into the yard and tried to forget the girl. I held the note in my hand, and it brought a smile to my face.

"Still got it."

CHAPTER
TWELVE

THE MORNING COMMUTE in LeClaire was nonexistent. A five-mile jaunt up Highway 24, left on Main, and three blocks to Darby Road. Arrive at Antique Adventures. One benefit of a small town is a small chance of road rage.

I reached into the glove box, pulled out a pipe, and tried to not spill the coffee between my legs. The warmth of the travel mug felt soothing on my thighs.

I took out a small plastic bag from my red flannel shirt pocket. I squeezed my thighs together, trying to keep the coffee from spilling while using my elbow to keep the steering wheel straight.

I dropped a pinch of marijuana into the skull-shaped pipe bowl. The truck-issued cigarette lighter popped out like a Jack in the Box. I jammed the glowing red tip on the bowl.

I sucked in on the pipe like it was my last.

A calmness surged though my body, like everything was okay in the world.

I rolled the windows down to banish any evidence of my habit and to calm any reminders of my sad life during the day. A spray of Binaca after the fact would complete the job.

The Ford F-150 truck rolled up on the gravel driveway. I

dumped the remnants of ash on the ground, smelled my clothes, and headed toward the glass door entrance of Antique Adventures.

The door swung open, and Maria emerged in front of my face, cursing in Spanish under her breath. "The phone is for you. It's the bank telling us we have thirty days to pay our mortgage. They are going to take our shop. Did you know about this?"

I grabbed the phone, knowing the mortgage was late, and tried to settle down the worked-up Mexican. "Hello, this is Dexter. I'm the owner."

"Mr. O'Kane, we noticed you are months behind in your mortgage. We have sent multiple notices by mail and email. We need a payment soon or we will be looking at foreclosure."

I paced around the office, looking to the sky, hoping money would fall from the clouds. "I'm sorry. Things are not good right now for the business. I did get the correspondence and have been wanting to get back to you. Life has been busy. You know how it is."

The woman on the line became compassionate for a moment and switched back to stern. "I know life gets busy. But, we are going to need at least one month's payment of your mortgage in thirty days before we take legal action."

I tugged on my black hair and continued to pace around the cold office. I felt like a failure with every call from the creditors. I sat in my swivel chair and stared at a family picture given to me for Father's Day. The frame said #1 Dad.

"Okay. I will do my best. I will try and get you the money in thirty days."

The mortgage woman gave me the options for payment. I was not listening. "Mr. O'Kane … Mr. O'Kane, you still there? Is there anything else we can help you with?"

"Yeah. Okay. Will do." The phone went dead.

I left the office to see Maria standing behind the counter, nursing a coffee, her eyes looking tired.

"What am I supposed to do if I lose this job? Go back to being a waitress. I have three kids to feed."

I walked over to the glass cases, leaned on them with both arms, and tenderly looked into Maria's eyes. "We are going to get this figured out. Every business goes through rough patches. I will not lose this business; everything will be okay. I promise."

I knew the words leaving my mouth were not true.

Maria was part of my family. Her husband bailed on her two years ago for another woman. We helped with some bills and babysat her children when she needed to work. Spencer loved playing with her youngest son, George. I did everything possible to pay her a good wage. I know what it's like to see a dad leave their family. Mine left when I was six.

I waved Maria to come closer. I gave her a hug. "We are going to be okay. You are family. We will get through this together."

She leaned back and examined my bloodshot eyes. "You look funny Mr. O'Kane. Everything okay?" she asked.

"I am fine. Just tired," I said, pushing her away.

I walked back to my cold and quiet office, shoulders slumped over like I'd lost the Super Bowl. The calmness of a marijuana-induced high was replaced by panic of losing the business and the people I love.

I slumped into the swivel chair, laid my head on the desk, and began to weep. I turned on the radio to shield Maria from the tears.

My phone made a pinging sound. It was Samantha Rose.

Call me, her message read. *We need to talk.*

CHAPTER
THIRTEEN

I ATE lunch with John and Maria, trying to forget the pressure of paying a mortgage with money we didn't have. I stuffed fries in my face and didn't say much to the other two.

Maria handed me a piece of paper. "I found a pick thirty miles from here. It's a township called Marshall. The person who lives here is interested in trading. Please don't screw this up. We need this… white boys."

Antique Adventures had a good reputation in the antique and picker community. When other collectors saw something they wanted in the shop, they proposed a trade. Rusty gold for rusty gold. The equivalent of "you scratch my back, I'll scratch yours".

Trades make me nervous. Most collectors try and rip us off with uneven trades. Thinking they know the market better than me. I have too many picks under my belt to be the fool.

Trades can be an avenue of a quick score. Or, leave an item on the shelf in the shop worth beans.

I placed the piece of paper in my pocket and gave Maria a high five. "We got this. Our hands will be filled with treasure. You'll see," I said, not feeling as confident as my words expressed.

Maria munched on a burger and then wiped her mouth before the ketchup could fall on the table.

"I got babies to feed, Dex," she said, picking up a fry.

We hopped in the van and headed north on Highway 24 toward Marshall, Missouri, a small township not far from LeClaire, founded after the Civil War. The thousand-person township was filled with dusty back roads, farmhouses, and barns filled with junk to the ceiling. The kind of place pickers dream about.

John broke the silence, reaching down into the center console, pulling out a black vial. He held it to my ear. "Check this out. I've been working on a new experiment."

John attended Missouri State and spent his first two years studying Biology and Chemistry. He dreamed of being a doctor, or at least a lab rat. After getting asked to leave school for an underground poker ring, he now used his untapped potential to come up with new potions. Being single gives him the time.

I held the mystery substance up to the light piercing through the truck. "What is it? Looks like oil for my truck."

John ripped the vial back out of my hands and held it in his palm. "This, my friend, is the future for killing deer."

John grew up in a hunting family. Every open season, his father, brother, and anyone in LeClaire with a rifle were invited to kill stuff. The combination of singleness and too much time on his hands led to this. Hunting animals and creating elixirs.

"Killing deer? Tell me more," I said.

"I figured out a way to kill a deer without a gun. A couple dabs of my special sauce, and anything a deer touches or licks will put him down in a couple minutes."

John is constantly looking for the easiest way to do something. John is not lazy, but always looking for an edge. Like starting a gambling ring, because filling out financial aid forms was too much work.

"I am scared to ask. How do you know this will kill a deer?"

John's folds of fat on his large midsection began shaking from laughter. "Let's just say there are many dead squirrels littered around the house," he said.

I gave a slow head shake, knowing John was bored. "How do you know it will work on a deer? Isn't a deer going to need more of your potion to lay him down?" I asked.

"Of course, that might seem like a problem to the laymen. The simple answer is … you up the dosage based on the size of animal. It is a simple formula based on weight."

"How are you going to know how much the animal weighs?"

John ignored the question and shook the vial. "I have not tested this on a deer. I am confident it will work."

I stole back the potion and closed it inside the middle console. "Let's forget about the deer poison and focus on our next pick. We need fast cash, or we are screwed."

John's face became deflated. He said in a quiet tone, "I know Maria knows more than me. How bad is it? Are we going to lose the business?"

"Don't worry about that. We just need to make some money and we'll be fine."

The layers of lies put a pit in my stomach.

CHAPTER
FOURTEEN

THE TRUCK RUMBLED up to a large, white, two-story farmhouse. The yard was immaculately layered with flowers, fresh cut green grass, mulch, and gnomes. Not a good sign.

A fruitful pick typically involves refrigerators on the lawn, 1967 Ford Mustangs on blocks, and boarded-up, rotting barns. The more distraught the yard, better the odds.

I glanced to the right of the farmhouse and saw a half dozen-long row of sheds. Relief.

I walked up the wide, wooden steps to the large, white house and knocked on the door. John caught his breath behind me.

"Really? Five steps and you're out of breath."

"I'm carrying a little holiday weight," John said, bent over and gasping for breath.

"Which holiday? Christmas of 1987?" I said, with a grin.

The front door rattled open and an elderly gentleman smiled through the screen door. He pushed the door open and looked up from a hunched position.

"You the boys from Antique Adventures come to trade with me? Name's Reginald." The man was missing two bottom teeth.

John reached out his hand. "Yes, we're the guys, old-timer. Can we take a look around? Name's John; his name is Dexter."

The man pushed both of us aside and shuffled down the steps. He dragged his feet like they had fallen asleep. He pointed toward a large barn in the distance. "Let's start with that one."

John and I smiled at one another, amazed at the agility of the old-timer. We walked over to the barn and helped the old man open the large sliding doors.

The doors opened, and the smell of dust and mildew punched us in the nose.

John sneezed.

I stood in awe of the wall-to-wall shelves and piles of rusty gold in every corner of the barn. Bona fide, rusted-out, beautiful junk. We hid behind the old man, gave high fives, and tried to contain ourselves.

Score.

Too much excitement can work against a fruitful pick. The seller doesn't appreciate an overconfident buyer. If they think you are going to rip them off or low-ball them, they might not sell you a thing.

John likens it to the Poker Face. Don't tell 'em your hand with your face.

We began to pick, and the feeling of momentum surged through my body. For the first time in a long time, I was confident we could make some cash and begin chipping away at the debt. I imagined our financials moving from the red to the black.

I wrangled from a pile of rusted items a large Texaco sign, and held it up to the old man. "How 'bout a trade for this sign?"

With a moment of hesitation, he pondered the exchange, scratching a white beard. "Nope."

"I was thinking an old Shell Oil sign, straight up?" I shot back.

"No way, kid. That sign means a lot to me. One of the first signs I ever picked. I can't give it away for a Shell Oil sign. Texaco is worth more," he said.

"You think Shell is worth less than Texaco? You're crazy."

The old man ignored me.

John jumped into the game with another item. "How about this?" he asked, pointing down to a rusted-out, turn-of-the-century bicycle. "I got a similar one in the shop."

"Um, what kind, and year?"

"Schwinn, I think. 1923."

"Nope. My bike is worth more. Schwinn is American, and mine is from Europe."

John looked over at me and mouthed, "What?" he shot back. "No way a Schwinn is inferior to this European model. That is a fair trade."

The old man moved a sign and lamp to another shelf. "No. That bicycle belonged to my father. He rode it around in England during the war."

An hour after haggling, negotiating, and pleading. The writing on the wall.

What is the fear of every picker? The emotionally-attached collector. No amount of haggling, coercing, or pleading will change the mind of a sentimental collector. Their minds are made up long before you ever arrive for a pick.

They like the idea of making money. Emphasis on the word *like*. When push comes to shove, they would rather die with a barn full of junk than make a few bucks.

The reality began to set in. A sadness brewed in my stomach, thinking about Maria back at the shop.

We are dead.

A failed pick.

No cash. No trades. Nothing.

We drove back to the shop and did not say a word.

CHAPTER
FIFTEEN

A RUMBLING soul matched the rumbling truck marching down Highway 24. An emotional concoction of confusion, anger, and loss brewed in my blood. The haunting thoughts of a failing business. Loss of family. A failed pick. I knew of one solution.

I reached down into the glove box and pulled out the skull pipe. I maneuvered the small plastic *dime* bag and gently pushed a pinch full down into the bowl.

I glanced over at John, watching his eyes widen at my preparation.

"I don't care what you think of me right now. I need a smoke. You were going to find out sooner or later."

I jammed the lighter in the bowl, took a deep breath, and felt the immediate calm of narcotics coursing through my body.

John shook his head and looked over with his mouth hanging open in disbelief. "How long have you been sucking on the skull pipe?"

I was surprised by the calm tone John used to confront my habit. I blew smoke out of the passenger window and peeked back at John.

"Shortly after Spencer and Lisa died. I met a guy at O'Malley's. Told me he smoked for medicinal purposes. A busted-up back. We smoked a bowl in the parking lot, and the rest is history."

John shook his head in disappointment, like a mother correcting a wayward child. His eyes were sad. "Marijuana? Really? I would never peg you as the hippie type. If anyone would spoke pot, it would be me," he said with a short grin.

"I am not a hippie. But, sometimes, gotta do whatever I can to get me through the day. I need this after another failed pick."

John sipped his Cherry Coke. You could see the wheels spinning in his mind as he searched for his next words.

"So… is this a phase? Are you going to stop?"

I took another hit and blew concentric circles out the window. "We'll see. This stuff is my functional counselor. It helps with the pain."

"I understand you are hurting because of your family and business trouble. Maybe you need to see a real counselor. Not vapors from the mouth of a skull pipe."

"You understand—" I tapped on the glass of the passenger window. John saw what I saw: a row of barns on the side of the highway, and rusted-out vehicles. He pulled off at the exit.

I directed John toward a driveway next to the barns and rusted gold.

John yanked the wheel, almost flipping the van. He headed north down a narrow gravel road, toward a small house in the woods. The pot holes in the gravel road bounced the van up and down. Cherry Coke and hot marijuana ash spilled in the cockpit of the van.

"Maria told me about a place in this area. A backup pick in case things went bad," John said.

"Slow down, big fella. The house is up on the right. Let's freestyle this one and try to make up for a lost day."

John gave me the nod, slammed the brakes, and we slid on the gravel road.

"That was fun," I said.

I grabbed a flyer and sprayed my clothes with deodorant, trying not to smell like a hippie after Woodstock. We jogged up to the house while I sprayed Binaca in my mouth. I peered into an open window on the right.

I gave a gentle knock. Waited for an answer. I scanned the surrounding yard to see the potential. I was hopeful.

I knocked again. No answer.

I noticed the lock slightly unhinged from the door. I gave a gentle push and the door opened. I looked back at John to get a confirmation.

"Hello, anyone home? My name is Dexter O'Kane, and I wanted to see if you are selling today."

Nothing.

A thud, like a child jumping from a bunk bed, rang out from the back of the house.

"Hello? Is anyone here?"

I tiptoed through a living room and peeked left down a hallway looking for signs of life. The wooden floor creaked under my work boots, making my heart get nervous.

A side bedroom door jolted open. A bearded man ran out of the room and headed for the back of the house. I yelled at him, "Stop. You the owner of the house?"

The residue of my marijuana high made the man a twin. I tried to shake the cobwebs from my vision. The mystery man ran through a screen door, out into the backyard.

I wiped my eyes, trying to get a better look.

I ran to the screen door and watched the man disappear into the woods.

John came up behind me. "What's going on? Was that the owner? Where did he go?"

"I don't know. Whoever it was, he got scared."

I turned back into the house, and became very aware that we just trespassed into a stranger's place. "Let's get out of here. This does not look good."

We paced back down the hallway, trying to make it out of the house. A bedroom door was cracked open and I casually looked in. A pool of blood expanded out like ice turning to water on the wooden floor. A woman lay in the middle, her throat slit up the side and her eyes wide open.

I looked up at John. "We got a problem."

CHAPTER
SIXTEEN

WE STOOD OVER THE BODY, looking down at the pool of blood growing on the floor. Redness still colored her olive cheeks. Hair and blood mingled in the dirty bedroom.

I shook my head, stunned.

John turned toward me with pale face trying to find comprehendible words. "So... um... this can't be good."

The haze of a marijuana high began to lift as adrenaline pumped through my veins. I inspected the body with an odd fascination. Didn't know why this woman intrigued me.

"I didn't get a great look at the killer. But, he had a beard like our killer at Ford's place. People are dropping like flies in LeClaire. I am tired of it."

John's eyes froze wide with shock. "You think this is the same guy? The chance of seeing two murders in LeClaire, a couple days apart—we should go to Vegas with these odds."

I smiled, still locked on the dead woman on the floor. She was probably only twenty-five. "I think God, the Sky Ferry, Man Upstairs, he or she, or *it*, is messing with us. Probably divine punishment of sorts."

John hit me in the arm. "Stop messing around. I don't think

God cares about a couple pickers in a nobody town in Missouri. He's got better things to do."

I rubbed my chin and scratched the side of my cheek. "Why do we keep seeing these murders? Someone is trying to get our attention," I said.

John peeked out of the bedroom window to see the surroundings. "I don't want to get mixed up in this, Dex. Let's leave the body and get out of here. No one knows we've been here. The closest neighbor is miles away."

I paused to think about the proposal, knelt down next to the body, and reached over to the bed. I placed a white sheet over the woman's silent corpse. "She still has a name. She's someone's daughter. Now we can go."

We sprinted back through the house, out the screened porch, jumped back in the truck, and sped off. I frantically grabbed my phone and called Maria.

"Maria, don't get mad. We're coming back to the shop empty handed. But, something happened and I can't talk about it right now."

"You better have gotten mauled by a bear or I don't want to hear it," Maria shot back.

"Not a bear. But not good."

Maria hung up the phone. *Ay, ay, ay,* I thought. *What am I going to do?*

I sat in the van staring out the window, replaying the image of the dead woman in my mind. I don't know why there was a seedling of fascination stirring up in me. *Was it someone I knew? Is something or someone trying to get my attention? Was I to stop the killings?*

The humming of tires on the highway mixed with strange ideas and feelings. I broke the silence. "I want to find the man who killed this woman. He probably killed Ford, too. We need to do something."

The words coming out of my mind and mouth felt right in the moment. They were confident words.

John chuckled as his rolls of fat waved up and down. John held a swollen paw in my face.

"Easy there, Columbo. Haven't we talked about this already? There's nothing we can do. We happened to be in the wrong place at the wrong time. It's time to move on. We need to focus on getting the business back on track."

I was not satisfied with pretending things were going to be okay. I needed this on some kind of cosmic level.

"No. The person who killed Ford, and possibly this woman, needs to be stopped. We know just as much as the authorities. We will stop him. That is the new plan," I said, slapping my hands together.

I rummaged through the center console and pulled out the black vial of deer poison. I pushed it in John's face. "You think this could kill a human?"

"Slow down, Dex. We're not killing anyone. This poison is a hobby to kill animals. Not people. You've lost your mind."

I felt my focus shift to the idea of finding and killing this man. There was an almost robotic feel to the idea. I could not think of anything else in the world. "We will destroy the bearded man. That is the new plan."

John raised an eyebrow and peeked at me. "Is that marijuana making you hallucinate? You sound like a crazy person."

"I don't know what I feel right now. This is the new plan."

I turned the poison over in my hand and held it in the sunlight shooting through the van window.

John snatched the poison out of my hand. "No! We are not killers. Let it go, Dex. Snap out of it."

I rarely see John get worked up because of his laid-back and fun-loving persona. But when he feels strongly about something, he will respond. I knew my plan was ludicrous. Yet, it sounded right.

"I don't care anymore. Our town does not need all this killing going on. It's time we stop being pansies and start doing something about our situation. This is the new plan…"

Silence filled the van.

I could feel the resistance between John and me on the ride home. I needed to do something. I was not exactly sure *how* or *what*. But, I needed to act.

The woman in the pool of blood deserved that.

CHAPTER
SEVENTEEN

POP. POP. POP. The sounds of gunfire ricocheted through my trees in the yard.

"Holy crap. This thing has kick," I yelled out like an excited kid on Christmas.

I leveled the Beretta .92 up to my eye, steadied my hand, and focused on makeshift targets of cans sitting on the fence. One-by-one, the cans fell dead on the ground.

My dog Murphy lay on the porch, head raising after every shot, his sad eyes wondering what was going on with his master.

I practiced shooting with intensity in my bones. Not sure why the gun felt right and good. I enjoyed the control the gun gave me. Like I was accomplishing something.

My pants began to vibrate. I tried to ignore it, but it was no use.

Concentration lost.

I examined the phone, staring at the caller ID: Samantha Rose. I wiped my sweaty hands and a smile built up on my face. I thought about the night at the bar.

"Hello, this is Dexter."

"Why didn't you call me?" she asked, her voice a mixture of sweetness and angst.

"You're the one who left me a letter. Why didn't you call me? I thought we were one and done," I shot back with a smile.

"True. I wanted to tell you thanks for being a gentleman that night. I don't meet guys like you very often."

"You caught me on a good night. I'm usually awful."

"I don't believe it. So what you doing now?" Samantha asked.

I hesitated, not sure if guns were her thing. "Nothing. Sitting on the porch with Murphy, my dog."

A pause. "You need company?"

I gave an invisible fist pump and imaginary high five to the dog, trying to stay composed.

"Sure. I don't have anything going on."

"Cool. I'll be over in about an hour. See you then."

Lisa was the only woman I had ever been with. Other than small crushes in grade school, I didn't know how the dating thing worked. The thought of Samantha coming over made me nervous.

I fired off rounds for a few more minutes, watching the cans explode upward and down to the dirt. I thought about Samantha. Then, I thought about Lisa, feeling like I was cheating on her. I knew there would come a point to move on. Maybe this was the time.

I petted Murphy on his brown fur. "Not bad, old boy. Nailed every can."

Murphy rolled over and did not seem interested in my skills.

"You wouldn't know a sharp shooter if it jumped up and bit you," I said with confidence.

I stared intently at the shiny Beretta. Light bounced off its perfect black body. I positioned it tightly in my hand and pretended to shoot the bearded man.

The *new plan* danced in my mind. I didn't know all the details. Not sure what this meant. But, I felt desperate, and needed to take control. I needed to fix the mess of my life.

I waved Murphy over to me. "Come on, boy. Daddy's got a special friend coming over. I need to wash up."

I placed the Beretta in a black leather case and set on a top shelf in my bedroom. The case laid next to my discharge papers from the Navy.

Thoughts of the *new plan* were elbowed out by a beautiful woman coming over to see me. That was unexpected.

CHAPTER
EIGHTEEN

AN HOUR LATER, a red Ford Focus pulled into the driveway of my small wooden cabin in the country. A blonde with long, skinny legs walked up the steps to the porch.

Every time I saw Samantha, I could not help but think of Lisa. Probably the reason I was attracted to her.

"Hey stranger. How you been?" Samantha said with a large, white-toothed grin.

I hesitated, knowing I couldn't be fully honest. I ruminated on the murders and failing business. "Okay. I've been better."

Samantha pressed in on me. Her perfume wafted in my nose. Fruity.

My body felt nervous as she gave me an unexpected hug. She whispered in my ear, "I hope that tonight you will forget about whatever is troubling you."

I held her a beat too long. Probably giving off a desperate vibe. "Thanks."

I turned her around and placed both hands on her eyes. I gently guided her up the steps, onto the porch. I released my hands from her eyes.

There was a small, round table with a white tablecloth and a simple candle burning in the middle. The steam from a plate of spaghetti and meatballs floated into the night air.

"Ah. Did you cook for us?" Samantha said, turning red.

"Don't get too excited. It's been years since I've made spaghetti. The bachelor life does not lend itself to fine dining. Eat at your own risk," I said, pouring her a glass of red wine.

"I bet it tastes wonderful."

We sat and enjoyed our pasta, drinking, laughing, and telling stories. In the middle of our conversation. Samantha got serious and looked up at me with intense eyes.

"Dexter. There's something I need to tell you. I'm not assuming our relationship will go further than tonight. But, I need to be upfront about something."

I ate the last piece of garlic bread and chewed slowly. "Go ahead. I won't bite."

"I have a daughter. A six-year-old named Lisa. My husband died of cancer a few years ago. I'm not sure why I needed to tell you this. But now you know."

I swallowed hard on my last bite. I felt connected to her in a fresh way. I wasn't ready to share my story. I didn't know why, but the timing was off.

Samantha sipped her wine. "Uh oh. You're quiet. Did I freak you out?"

"I'm fine. Just taking it all in."

"Did my daughter scare you?"

"Of course not. I love children. I'm sorry about your husband. I feel like death is all around these days."

"Huh?"

"Nothing. I seem to be hearing many sad stories of late. That's all.

"Thank you for caring. It means a lot. We're getting by... it's hard. I am not even sure why I'm here. This might be too soon." Samantha sat up and her napkin fell to the floor. She began to tear up. "I probably should leave."

I grabbed her hand, pulled her gently back down into the

chair, and looked into her deep, blue eyes. "I want you here. I'm fine."

We talked, laughed, and drank wine for the rest of the evening. I felt safe with Samantha. A safety not felt in some time.

The one question I feared during the evening. "I've done all the talking. What's your family like? Ever been married, kids?"

"Nope. Never been married. No kids," I said.

CHAPTER
NINETEEN

THE MORNING MIST fell on the quiet streets of LeClaire. John pulled into the driveway to pick me up for work. He got out of the truck and smiled at the woman fixing her hair in the doorway. Samantha tugged at her ear, trying to correct a crooked earring.

John gave her an *I know what you did last night* smile as she got in her car.

"It's not what you think. What's your name? I don't think we've met." Samantha held out her hand and blushed.

"My name is John. I'm Dexter's best friend. I approve all active relationships," he answered, giving her a smirk.

"Samantha Rose. I'm a friend of Dexter, too."

"Friends? Friends with benefits?" John asked.

"Wow. I have not heard that one since high school. Just friends. You have a good day. Hope the picking goes better today," Samantha said, and got into her car and drove off down the dusty road.

John nodded.

I ran down the porch steps, trying to put on my jacket. "Don't start with me. Nothing happened. We're just friends."

John leaned up against the truck with a smug look on his face. "So, I've heard. She seems nice."

"Samantha came over last night for dinner, we drank a bit, and she slept on the couch. I didn't want her driving home because she lives on the other side of town."

John held up both hands. "You don't have to explain yourself. You're a big boy," he said.

"Let's go. We need to make money today. The timeline is getting tight before the creditors take the business."

John reached down to turn on the radio. A man's voice came on.

"Yesterday, a woman was found off Highway 24 dead in her home. The cause of death, possible homicide. Nothing conclusive at this point. Police are working to find a suspect. If you have any information, please contact LeClaire PD."

We glanced at one another.

"Last night, I was working in my lab," John said.

I paused, snorted. "Ah, yes. The mad scientist lab. What are you working on these days?"

"Knock it off. I take my experiments seriously. "

"Sorry, big fella. I know you hate when I make fun, Mr. Science Home Lab."

John, almost embarrassed to speak the next words, tried to spit them out. "I've been thinking about what you said the other day. When you asked about the poison being able to kill people. And, you know… the *new plan*."

I pushed on John's arm and laughed. "Don't listen to me. I wasn't serious. I'm in a bad place and searching for answers. I hate knowing these killings are happening in LeClaire, the town I love. You're right, what are we going to do anyway?"

That appeared to anger him. "No, Dexter. I'm serious. I've been thinking about the plan. I came up with a poison that might help."

"The same stuff for killing deers?"

"Yep. I'm tweaking the dosage for larger mammals. A way to kill humans in a humane and painless way."

The conversation intrigued me. "Are you saying if someone were to touch or swallow the poison, they would not feel it? Die peacefully? How do you know for sure?"

"I've been testing this stuff on mice. My research confirms it works. The mice do not suffer and die peacefully after a few minutes of exposure to the poison," John said.

"These are mice. Humans?"

"It's a simple tweak of potency. Piece of cake."

"I'm curious. Why does it matter how people die? What if the people deserved to die in a horrible way?" I asked.

John's tone became gentle. "Dex. We're not murderers. We don't want to torture people. We just want justice in LeClaire, right?"

I scratched my head, trying to figure out where the conversation was going. "Wait a minute. You want to find the killer and use poison to take him down. In a humane way, of course."

John avoided eye contact with me, fidgeting with his hands. "I don't know what I'm saying. Last night in my lab I kept thinking about the *new plan*. I couldn't sleep. I'm trying to figure out what this means, too."

I reached down into a black bag on the floor and pulled out my Beretta .92.

"I've been thinking about the plan too. Last night before Samantha came over, I got out my gun, and shot cans in the yard. I felt a need to. Something drew me to it."

"What does this mean, Dex?" John asked.

"I can't say for sure. But, we need to explore this further."

CHAPTER
TWENTY

WE DROVE up to the shop and were greeted by Maria reading a newspaper on a bench. She held up the paper and handed it to me.

The headline read: LECLAIRE AREA KILLER STRIKES AGAIN.

My eyes widened, reading more. "The killer of Ford, the woman at the house, and another man, seem to be part of the same family. They still don't have many leads."

John piped in with a snort, "That's not surprising. There's a lot of inbreeding going on in LeClaire. We don't have family trees. We have wreaths."

I stared John down, giving him a *you are dumb* kind of look. "So, the bearded killer has issues with a particular family. Interesting." I skimmed down and then turned to the next page. "Oh, crap. The killer might be related to the victims. But, yet to be determined. I would hate to be part of that family reunion."

"Sounds like the killer is out for revenge. You gotta deal with that stuff or it will kill ya," John said.

Maria knocked the paper out of my hand. She put her hands on her hips and stared both of us down.

"Who cares? There is nothing we can do. Let the police

handle it. You white boys need to get on a pick and make money. Or, I'm going to be waiting tables at Mel's again."

"You're right. What do you have for us today? Anything juicy? We are on a cold streak."

Maria rolled her brown eyes. She handed me a piece of paper with an address. "Even you guys can't mess this one up. An estate sale."

Estate sales are every picker's dream. Someone dies, the family is left with a pile of old crap, and wants to sell low. The people running the sales are either hired from the outside and have no emotional investment, or they are family members who are emotionally fragile and aren't looking to make a profit.

If a picker can get in on an estate sale, the prospect for piles of cash are high. At this point, we needed to be on our *A* game.

I high fived John and we yelled in unison. "Estate sale. Score!"

I settled into the passenger seat of the van and felt my phone begin to vibrate.

"This is Dexter."

"Dexter, we need to talk. Something bad happened."

"Are you okay?"

"I'm fine. But, we need to talk now." It sounded like Samantha was crying.

CHAPTER
TWENTY-ONE

JOHN DROVE east down Highway 7, heading out of LeClaire. He was giddy about the estate sale and didn't know Samantha was on the phone.

"What's going on?" I asked.

Samantha choked back tears and spoke in choppy sentences. "Something bad happened. Another family member was killed yesterday."

A fog of past memories swirled in my head. The pain of losing Lisa and Spencer resurfaced from her words. The idea of *another family member* didn't register for a moment.

Who else died?

My memory came back and drifted to the first time we met in the bar. *Samantha was crying about the loss of a family member.*

"I'm so sorry, Samantha. Where are you?"

"At home. I need you to come over. There's something I want to talk to you about," she said, in between sobs.

I began to feel anxious, knowing we needed this pick. The idea of Maria's wrath at the shop was enough to scare me straight. Time was running out and we didn't need any more sideways energy.

I hesitated, and tried to barter with Samantha. "Um, don't take this the wrong way. Can we meet up later? I'm at work and can't get away."

I waited for the bomb to drop. "No problem. Why don't I come to you? I really need to talk," she said with a sense of urgency in her voice.

"Okay," I said.

I picked up the piece of paper with the estate sale address and read it. "I'll see you in a bit." I hung up the phone.

John peeked over at me. "Everything okay on the home front?"

I twirled the phone and didn't want to tell John. "That was Samantha. She needs to talk. Someone in her family died last night."

"That's heavy."

"I never told you this. The night Samantha and I met, a different family member died. She was torn up over it."

He nodded in agreement. "Well, yes. When someone dies, that's usually normal," John said.

I knew John didn't make the connection. "Did you hear what I said? This is a different family member that died. Two people in the last two weeks. Get it?" I said.

"Wow. That's weird. I guess it happens, but weird."

"Of course it's weird. LeClaire has a population of 20,000. When multiple homicides happen close together, people take notice. You think Samantha's family is connected to the bearded killer?" I asked.

"Anything's possible. You barely know the chick," John said.

"She's going to meet me at the estate sale. I will find out more," I said.

I was breaking the number one rule of picking. Mixing business and pleasure. The picker must be focused on the job or the chance of losing thousands of dollars becomes a reality. I knew inviting Samantha to the sale might be a regret. But, I knew she needed me right now.

"No way. You know the rules. We need a big score on this sale. If not, you are going to feel the wrath of Maria, and lose the business," John said, his neck turning red.

I slapped John across his broad back. "No worries. It will be fine. She's having a tough time, we'll talk, and show this estate sale who's boss."

John peered at me with venom in his eyes. "Don't screw this up. I'm not playing. If this goes bad, you can deal with Maria too. Picks before chicks. Don't forget."

I contemplated the connection of Samantha and the bearded murderer with her family. The thought sent butterflies into my stomach. I didn't know what to think of it all.

We arrived at the pick, greeted by a swarm of cars and people walking fast. I climbed over a woman on the porch eyeing a ceramic planter.

"Not good, Dex. Looks like it might be picked over. We need to work fast," John said in disgust.

In driving a car, they say you need to be on the defensive, watching for other cars and obstacles in your way. In picking, you are always on the offensive, the aggressor at all costs, knocking old people down at a crowded estate sale if needed.

John barreled through the crowded living room, scanning the room for a score. He picked up a crystal candy dish. A hand dangled from the handle.

"Excuse me, sonny. I'm going to buy this," a white-haired lady said with a scowl.

"I don't think so. I had it first," John shot back.

The lady released her frail hands from the dish and placed them on her hips. "Not a very nice way to treat your elders," she said.

"I don't have time for this, ma'am. My partner and I need this more than you know." John looked back at me.

I waved and smiled, enjoying the entire scene. "Hey, big fella. I'm going to see if Samantha is here. Looks like you need to work this out," I said, leaving the room.

I stood at the front door, trying to look at the sea of people in the front yard. Samantha's red car came into view. I skipped down the hill to meet her.

I gave her a hug and whispered in her ear, "I am sorry for your loss."

I felt Samantha begin to give small convulsions against my arms. "I don't understand. This is too much to take. Whatever this is... it needs to stop," Samantha said, tears dripping from her cheeks.

The last words sent shock waves into my body. Like these words were personal. For me. My job was to stop whatever was happening in LeClaire.

Samantha pushed me back gently and stared with puppy dog eyes. "That's why I came. I need to talk to you about something."

I held my breath in anticipation of what she might say. *Maybe she is sick of me? Does she want to see other people?*

"I want to hire a professional. Someone to stop whoever is killing my family. The local police is a joke. I will pay anything."

"I know you are upset, but is this really what you want to do? I don't think you just look in the phone book for this kind of thing. The police are doing their best. What do you have in mind?"

Samantha scanned the property acting like she was under surveillance of some kind. She pulled me in close. "There's something you need to know. The person killing my family might be related to us. I have a distant uncle who moved away years ago who might be doing this."

I recalled the newspaper from earlier that day and made a connection. "The morning paper said the killings might be related. Same family. You think, distant uncle?" I asked.

"I don't know. My mother is confident he's the one. I am desperate."

I could sense the desperation and seriousness in her tone. "Who are you going to hire? You sound serious," I said.

"I don't know. But, I am going to do it soon. I am tired of this…"

I looked back up the hill, thinking about the earlier conversation with John. "I have the perfect people to help with this case. Let me get John and we will talk more."

CHAPTER
TWENTY-TWO

I LEANED against Samantha's red car, listening intently as she explained her strategy, while throngs of people rushed by, stacks of antiques in their arms.

The more I gazed into her eyes, the more I wanted to help. The more I listened to Samantha, the more I heard Lisa.

"The night we met at the bar, a family member had died. Frank Ford. He was an uncle. We weren't very close. Actually, most of our family are not close. Story for another day."

I held up my hand to Samantha's mouth trying to slow her speech. "Hold up. Did you say Ford?"

"Yes. Frank Ford was my uncle."

I shook my head in disbelief. "You're not going to believe this. John and I were on a pick. We witnessed a murder. The family who owned the house was named Ford. Could this be your uncle?" I asked.

Samantha paused, as if seeing a ghost. "You serious? A murder?"

"Serious as a heart attack. We saw the killer with our own eyes. And, we know the man who was killed is a Ford."

John came up smiling, hands full of antiques. He saved a

lamp from falling off the stack. "We scored." He examined Samantha and me. "What's going on? Why the long faces?"

I turned to John. "Tell Samantha who we saw get killed the other day."

"Which murder? The man or woman? Technically, we didn't see the chick get killed, but saw her bleeding out on the floor," John said.

Samantha spoke up, "You've seen more than one murder in the last week?"

"It's been a long couple of weeks," I said with a half-smile.

I helped John set the antiques on the ground before he shattered them to pieces. "What was the man's name? The guy we saw get his throat slit?" I asked John.

John paused, put a hand on his chin, and reached back into the recesses of his brain. "Uh, I think the name's Ford. Something Ford. George. Wilbur. Not sure."

"Told you," I shot back to Samantha.

Samantha massaged her neck, shuffled her feet, and stared at the ground. "You guys seem unmoved by these murders. You think murder is a joke?"

I grabbed Samantha on the shoulder and tried to console her. "We're not trying to make light of these murders or the pain you're in. The truth is, life has not been going well for me, of late. John either. We try and laugh these things off because life is laughable right now."

I knew I couldn't tell Samantha everything right now. I wanted her to know more of my story, but there was resistance.

Samantha stared at the ground to find her next words. "I don't know you guys that well. But, I need help. I want to find the person who is killing my family."

"Not to pry, but can you tell us who else died in your family? We've only heard about Frank," I asked.

"A couple days ago, my cousin Lily died. She lived on the east side of town, off Elm Street. The police found her dead body in her home. She was only twenty-five."

John and I shook our heads, knowing the area well. The same place where we saw the murdered woman, who looked about twenty-five. The connections and not-so-coincidences were beginning to make my head hurt.

"I think whoever killed Frank is probably the same person who killed your cousin," I said with confidence.

"Who would want to do a thing like this? Does someone have a grudge against someone in your family?" John asked.

"That's why I wanted to see you. I have a distant uncle named Jack Ford who disappeared about ten years ago. We assumed he was dead. But, now that these murders are happening, we think he might be involved."

"Why did he disappear?" I asked.

Samantha began to tear up, wiping her eyes with a tissue. "Jack disappeared when the family business went under. He had a successful used car company off Highway 24 in LeClaire. He wanted to hand the business over to my family when he retired. He began training some of the family to take it over. Unfortunately, right before retirement, none of the family wanted the business. They all walked away. He got bitter, blamed the family for his pain, and left without a trace."

"Did you ever meet Jack?" I asked.

"Vague memories. I was young when he left. Most of the family doesn't mention him much. Kind of a forgotten family member. Until now," she said.

I began to get nervous. The kind of nervous when you know you should do or say something, but not sure what. "So how can we help?"

"I'm not comfortable talking about this here in public. Can we meet up at your house? John can come, too…"

"Sounds like a plan," I said.

John and I got back in the van. I replayed the conversation with Samantha in my mind and it felt right. The connections I made with the killer and the satisfaction of helping someone in need, all good.

But I still didn't know exactly what we were getting ourselves into. I knew this killer needed to be stopped.

"What you thinking, Dex?" John asked, sipping on a Cherry Coke.

"Not sure. But, I know we need to help. I'm ready for something new. Something good to come our way," I said.

John reached behind the seat and pulled out a large vase and held it in my face. "Does this count for something good coming our way? Victorian era, probably worth $5000. Guess how much I paid for it?"

"Um… two thousand," I said.

"Not even close," John said, laughing.

"A thousand?"

"I stole it."

"What?"

"Considering the cold picking runs of late, we needed something to go our way. All that we've been through in the last couple months. We needed this one."

I hit John in his fat arm. "So, stealing a vase is your answer."

"Come on, man. The estate sale was packed. Old ladies were ripping stuff out of my hand. No one even saw me put it in my bag."

"If the police come and arrest your fat butt, I'm not bailing you out," I said.

Deep down, I didn't care all that much. Something was changing in me. The thought of theft and murder were no longer sacred things. They were becoming common vernacular and easier to speak of. *Maybe I need counseling? Maybe I am breaking down? Or maybe, just maybe, something good is on the horizon.*

"Don't worry. We're going to be fine. This is the start of something good," John said.

"I think you're right."

With a large grin, I peeked at the side mirror of the van. Samantha trailed close behind.

"I think you're right. You might *just* be right."

CHAPTER
TWENTY-THREE

NIGHT BEGAN to fall on my small cabin in the woods. Silence, with the occasional rustling of the trees.

We pulled up to the gravel drive and settled into the living room. Decorations, simple: pictures, and sparse furniture.

Simplicity was vital for the life of the bachelor with no domestic skills, and no desire to learn, for that matter.

I pointed to the couch. "Why don't you grab a seat? I'll bring drinks and snacks," I said, disappearing into the kitchen.

John and Samantha sat on the couch in silence. John broke the awkwardness by standing up, scanning the room, and trying to make small talk.

"I'm sorry about your family."

Samantha paused for a moment. "Thank you ... John ... is it?"

John nodded in agreement. "Sometimes I wish my mother named me something cool, like Fabio. Maybe I would've done something important with my life."

Samantha peeked up at John, looked around, and broke into laughter. "Fabio? That's good..."

"I'm serious. That guy has the hair, muscles, the tan. If I had

Fabio's physique, I might have had better luck with the ladies," John said, flexing a bicep.

"I don't think Fabio is the standard of a life worth living. You might want to think of a different bar."

"Batman?"

"Let's stop now," Samantha said.

Samantha and John bantered back and forth before I came back in the room.

I arrived with a tray of beers and BBQ chips. Bachelor food. "Sorry, all I got. Beggars can't be choosers," I said, placing the tray on the coffee table. I raised a beer, grabbed a palm full of chips.

John raised his bottle up.

"To good food. New friendships. New beginnings. Good things. Cheers," I said, clinking our bottles.

Samantha got down to business. "Let's talk about our strategy, what we began chatting about at the estate sale. I need to be honest … I don't know where we're supposed to start."

I got excited and leapt from my chair. She didn't know I had been thinking about this moment for some time. I grabbed Post-It notes, Scotch tape, and a pen from a small desk.

"I thought we could list all the details we have in place so far. All the people involved, when stuff happened, and any pertinent information. Samantha, tell me all the people involved one more time?"

I scribbled on the Post-It notes and stuck them on the wall. *People* on the first note. *Place* on another. *Time* on a third.

"The first murder was Frank. Which you guys witnessed." I wrote down *Frank* and filled in a couple details. I flashed back to the bearded man running into the woods. "We know Frank was killed by a bearded man. Possibly Samantha's distant uncle." I scribbled on *People,* and Ford's picking spot for *Place.*

Time, two weeks ago.

"If Samantha is right, Jack's motive is possibly revenge on the family revolving around the family business. We don't know for certain, but seems to make sense right now. You don't go around killing family members unless revenge is involved."

"Or, you're psycho," John said.

I continued to scribble on the Post-It notes. I hung another set next to the last ones. This one included the woman found dead in the house. "The second victim is the young woman. What's her name?"

"Lily. A cousin," said Samantha.

"How is she related to Jack? The distant uncle?" I asked.

"I think she's the daughter of Jack's cousin Roger. I don't think Lily could have anything to do with the business. She is too young," Samantha said.

"I think Jack might be trying to make a point. You mess with me, I kill everybody in the family," I said.

John and Samantha stared up at me like deer caught in headlights.

I walked around the room like a lawyer in court. I twirled my pen around in my right hand and then tapped it on my face. "So, we have a couple dead people. Possible suspect, the bearded man. Motive … failed business and family feud. Revenge is the name of the game."

Samantha held up both hands and waved them at me. "Okay, Columbo. Before we get ahead of ourselves. What are we"—she pointed to all of us—"going to do? I came here to figure out who to hire to stop Jack. Ideas?"

I pointed the ball-point pen at Samantha, squinted, and engaged her blue eyes. "Glad you asked. John and I have been discussing some ideas of our own. Not exactly a career change, but something along these lines. More of a side gig. We think a little change of scenery might be good right now," I said.

Samantha laughed. "What are you thinking? You guys are pickers and run an antique shop. I don't think I'm following."

I grabbed her arm, waved to John, and slammed the screen porch door open. I opened my truck, rummaged through a black bag, and emerged with my pistol.

I set the cans up on the fence. POP. POP. POP. Can after can fell dead to the ground. I spun the gun around in my hand like a gunslinger in the Wild West. "This is my plan."

"What? Shoot cans off a fence?" Samantha said with a smile.

I told them to grab a seat on the wooden chairs on the porch. I knelt down and got serious. "There's something I need to tell you both. Something in my past worth noting."

"The experimental phase in college?" John said, hitting Samantha's arm.

"No. After high school, I enlisted in the Navy. I went through basic training. Worked my way up and was being trained to be a sniper in the Navy Seals. A few weeks before being deployed to Iraq, I blew out my knee in a routine drill. It never healed right and that was the end of my career," I said.

"Okay," Samantha said.

John, in an excited moment, got up. "Oh shit. The MCL injury didn't happen in pickup basketball. You liar."

"I know. I was embarrassed, and did not want anyone to know that I flunked out of the Seals. I came back to LeClaire feeling like a failure. Only a few people know about this."

Silence blew through the yard.

"Okay, thanks for sharing, Dex. What does this mean?"

"I am a trained killer. I want to help."

CHAPTER
TWENTY-FOUR

SAMANTHA PACED the small living room. I could tell by the look in her eye she might be thinking differently about me. A trained killer. But I didn't see myself this way. I never went to battle. Never pulled the trigger. I didn't know if I was even capable of this kind of work. It was all in my head at this point. Only fantasy.

"I don't know. I appreciate the concern you have for LeClaire, me, my family. But, I don't know if this is a right fit for me. Maybe I should hire a hit man or something?"

I sensed the enthusiasm being sucked out of the room. I wanted this more than Samantha or John at this point. It was a risk. But, everything in life is a risk, isn't it? You don't know how things will turn out. I didn't think my family would end up in a grave. I needed this more than they knew.

"Let me try and sweeten the deal." I peered at John. "John's been working on some stuff related to this enterprise."

"What kind of stuff?" Samantha asked.

I whispered in John's ear to get the poison out of the van. "John is somewhat of a chemistry geek," I said to Samantha. "He's come up with a way to kill animals, or people, in a humane fashion. The goal is to eliminate suffering at all costs."

John rushed back into the house, carrying the small vial of black liquid. He handed it to Samantha. "We're not killers. We are a couple of guys trying to help the people of LeClaire. This stuff might be the answer we are looking for," John said.

Samantha shook the black substance and watched it rise and fall in the vial. She held it up to her face and examined it more closely. "I am not making the connection. This liquid is the answer to my problems and the murders of LeClaire? Isn't murder still murder, regardless of how you slice it?" Samantha asked.

I peered at John. "You're right, murder is murder. But when bad people do bad things to hurt innocent people, they need to be stopped. It's obvious our police department and local authorities are incompetent, and we think we can help."

Samantha got up from the couch, rubbed her temple, and paced around the living room. "I'm not sure about this. I thought you guys could give me guidance. I didn't think you were the ones to do the job. I need more time," she said.

I gave her a hug and reassured her of a *no pressure proposition*. "No problem, sweetie. We are on your side, whatever you decide," I said.

Samantha looked at her watch. "Crud. I need to get to the hospital. I am working the night shift tonight. I will call you later."

The red Focus sped off into the distance with red rear lights flashing in the dark of the night.

I looked over at John, and he sat silent, nursing a beer.

I wanted to end the LeClaire killer sooner than later. The patience and tenderness I showed to Samantha turned to impatience and anger.

"I'm going after this guy. If Samantha wants our help or not, he's going to be stopped soon. I promise you."

John raised an eyebrow at my response. But I knew him well enough that he was with me the entire way. He was loyal, and I needed loyal people in my life right now.

"Dex, whatever you decide, I'm in." He gave me a fist bump.

John sped off down the road in the van, and I grabbed a seat on a chair on the porch. I liked the new version of me. The evolving version of me. It felt like being born again.

I had no idea what this new version was all about, but I liked the potential.

I grabbed my Beretta sitting on a table, and began to fire at a circular target on a nearby tree. Every shot was within six inches of the bullseye.

CHAPTER
TWENTY-FIVE

THE NEXT MORNING, I pranced into Antique Adventures with new vibrancy and a sense of enthusiasm. A glimmer of hope not felt in a long time.

Maria looked me up and down, assuming I had lost my marbles. "What's up with you? It is good to see you with a smile. But, remember, there is not much to be happy with the biz, you know," she said.

I glided around the shop, picking up a variety of antiques... a vase, AM radio, Motorcycle gloves, and train light. "Some days are better than others. This is a good day," I said, dusting a shelf.

I thought about the *job* and the *new plan*. The new possibility and trajectory felt right. In the strangest possible rightness I could imagine. I didn't know why. I didn't want to know to be honest. I needed a purpose after losing the only thing I loved. The only people who made my life feel grounded and right, Lisa and Spencer. Finding the killer might be my salvation. Making right a wrong in the world.

"So, what you got for us today?" I asked Maria.

"Good work on the estate sale. The items John found are already beginning to sell. We need to keep the momentum going and get a few more profitable picks under the belt. If we want to get into the black, stay focused."

"Today will be a good day. I can feel it," I shot back.

Maria sat on a tall metal chair in front of an Apple computer, pecking at the keyboard. "I'll send an email with the directions and address to your phones. You're going to need GPS on this one. Kind of backwoods."

I loved the sound of backwoods. In the world of picking, the smaller the town, the better. The big cities most often left us high and dry. You need a lot of space to store rusty gold. Cities have limited space, not ideal for the picker.

"Have we worked with these folks before?" I asked.

"Nope. Fresh meat. Work your magic and get them on the *good list*," Maria said with a smile.

John came out of a back office. "No worries. He'll be in good hands. If I recall, the last pick was all me. Dexter was distracted by a special lady friend," John said, smacking me on the back.

Maria's face lit up. "Special lady friend... We can't have you distracted, white boy. Women and picking are bad combinations," Maria said.

"Picks before chicks," John said.

The thought of Samantha made me smile. My emotions were raw, and the idea of dating a woman, foreign. But whatever it was, it was nice.

"I'll be careful. I will not let it affect my work," I said.

"I know it's not my business, but you need to focus on *this* business right now. We need this, Dex," Maria said.

"I know. Got it."

We headed to the van. I opened the back of the white van doors, looked around to make sure no one was watching, and threw John a black jacket. "Try this on. It's a flak jacket. I had an old one, and picked one up for you."

John held the jacket up and looked at it with wide eyes. "You mean a bulletproof jacket?"

"Yep. Stop a bullet, or if a bomb goes off in your face. Don't worry, I got you an XXL, big fella," I said, laughing.

"Oh, more fat jokes. That's mature," John said.

"These are for the *new* business. I think we might need these in the future," I said, rubbing the slick, black material.

John put the back of his hand against his forehead and wiped a bead of sweat. "Are you sure about all of this? I thought about this last night, and it kind of freaks me out. I make poison in my basement. I don't know about tracking down killers," John said.

I didn't like John's response. I tried to keep my emotions in check and see his side. "Don't worry, big fella. I am probably going overboard. But, better safe than sorry," I said with a half grin. I threw the flak jackets back in the van and tried to ignore John's response for a moment. "Well, let's focus on the pick today. We need to get Antique Adventures back on track. We can worry about the *new* business later," I said.

"You're right. It does not hurt to be prepared when the time comes, right?" John said with a grin.

I bumped John's fist and felt my phone vibrate in my pocket. It was Samantha.

"Hey, Dex. It's me. I spent most of the night at work thinking about your offer. You got the job ... you and John," Samantha said.

I spun around in circles and gave John a high five. "Are you serious? This is great news. I will tell John."

"And, one more thing. I want to pay you."

I distanced myself from John and tried to use a quiet tone. "You don't have to pay us. You have a child to support. This one is free. We'll call it *pro bono* work," I said.

"The money is no problem. When my husband died, he left me quite a bit from the life insurance policy. This means a lot to me, and you are putting your life on the line. Please take the money," she said.

"I know what you mean, I can relate..."

"Huh?"

I couldn't let her know about Lisa, not yet. But, I now knew why there was an attraction to Samantha in quick fashion. We shared a common story. "Nothing."

"Will you take the money?"

"We will send you a bill later. I have no idea what this kind of work charges," I said with a smile.

The phone line went silent for five seconds. "Dexter, there is something I need to tell you. I like you. I don't know how that is possible after my first husband. But I don't want this to make our relationship weird. Whatever this relationship is," she said.

"Hiring me to be an assassin might make for interesting family dynamics. I understand. I will not make it weird, if you don't make it weird," I said.

Samantha gave a small giggle. "Yeah, your boyfriend killing a family member could made things awkward."

"Let's take it a day at a time and see where everything leads. That's my motto in life."

"Plan," she said.

I hung up the phone as John walked over. "Who was that?"

"Samantha. We got the job," I said.

"Is she going to pay us?"

"Of course. We don't kill for free."

CHAPTER
TWENTY-SIX

WE DROVE down Highway 24 with a renewed vigor for picking, life, and possible new business venture. Maria sent us to Lewisville, Missouri for a pick she was convinced would lead to more money. Lewisville was only a few miles outside of LeClaire and had proved fruitful in picks of the past.

I felt anxiety and pressure, knowing we needed solid picks to save the business and get back on track. But, I couldn't stop thinking about the potential of the *new business.*

John peeked at the GPS with a confused look on his face. "I hope Maria gave us a good address. These roads are sparse."

The GPS had been good to us when we drove the backroads of America. Unfortunately, most picking sites are not GPS-friendly.

John tapped on the small screen of the GPS, the van lurching up and down over the Missouri hillsides.

"I think we're getting close, but who knows?"

The GPS chimed in with a British woman's accent, "Turn left in 500 yards." John smiled at me.

"Thank you, Martha," John said, using one of our pet names for the GPS.

The van veered left, then right, and drove on a smooth

cement road, which later dipped down onto a gravel road. I liked what I saw. Gravel roads, farm houses, rusted-out cars piled on the side of the highway. Good signs for the picker.

We pulled up to a large blue house, and were greeted by a white three-car garage. Two large eagles sat atop matching posts in the yard. I felt their presence, like they were watching us.

I felt a pit in my stomach. The house looked too nice. The nicer the house, often, the worse the pick. "I'm not sure about this one, Dex," I said, pointing out the eagles. "Seems like a bust."

"You never know, big fella. Let's see what we got."

I half-jogged up to the house and knocked with a flyer in my hand. An older man, about sixty, opened the door and greeted me with a warm smile.

I handed him a flyer. "Hi, name is Dexter"—I pointed to John —"and my business partner, John. You talked to Maria, might be up for selling a few items. Here's a list of what we buy."

The heavyset older man peered down at the flyer and moved his glasses over his nose to get a better look. "I might be able to help you boys. Come around back and I'll show you what I got."

We followed the man around the side of the house to a red barn about a hundred yards from the house. The barn was surrounded by a dozen rusted-out classic cars begging to be picked. I stared at them, drool almost coming out of my mouth. I smiled at John. "Look at the rusty gold. I think one of those is a 1919 Ford Model T Coupe. These suckers are rare. We might have hit a gold mine," I said with a whisper.

The older man moved ahead of us and led the way. "Let's go and check out my barn. That's where most of my collection is. I think you'll like what you see."

The old man fidgeted with a rusty pad lock and swung open the large, red door. Walls upon walls of junk greeted our eyes. Bikes, signs, tools, lamps, toys, and any kind of rusted item you could think of. All ready for the taking.

I turned to the old man with wide eyes, putting on gloves and pulling out a flashlight. "Can we get started?"

The old man put out his hands. "It's all yours. Pick away."

I went to town, rummaging through boxes, scouring shelves, and climbing ladders trying to find an item to get the business back on track.

John grabbed an item and held it up to me, with a thumbs-up for "good job", calling out prices and haggling back and forth. The old man was gracious. Letting item after item go. He obviously wanted to make a dent after years of collecting.

Maria called me to check in and make sure the pick was going well. I kept it short. I couldn't be distracted while in pick mode. Sweat dripped from my head, hands slick and dirty from hunting for rusty treasure.

The old man excused himself and left the barn for a few minutes. John watched him leave and didn't think much of it. We continued to dig, unaware of the surrounding world.

A *thump*.

I perked up and looked at John. "Did you hear that bump? It sounded like something hit against the barn."

John nodded and worked at a pile of rusted toys stacked up on the dirt floor.

"The owner left a few minutes ago. Maybe he is doing something outside."

Thump.

It sounded like something was bumping against the east wall of the barn. I decided to leave the pick and see where the sound was coming from. I waved at John, who was deep in pick mode.

"I'm going to see what's going on outside."

I walked slowly out of the barn doors and looked left and then right, not noticing anything unusual. A bird flew overhead that caught my eye, an eagle. I glanced up, in awe of its massive wings and serious face.

I got lost in the face of the eagle and heard the bump again around the back of the barn. I peered left and glided slowly to the back. "Hello, Mr. Washington, are you back here? I heard a noise and wanted to make sure everything's okay."

I made my way to the back of the barn and the old man was sliding slowly down the side of the barn, blood pouring down his face, eyes wide open. A bearded man stood over his body, peering at the five-inch slice down the side of Mr. Washington's neck. He had a look of satisfaction.

My hands trembled as I tried to speak. The killer spoke first, aiming the knife in my direction. "Don't say a word or you will be next. You'll bleed out like a stuck pig."

The intense blue eyes, slender, small body, and gray beard greeted my soul, turning it to rage. I knew this was the killer of Frank and the woman. The slight grin of a man who knows what he's doing and enjoying it. I can never forget this face.

I slipped my right hand around the back of my pants and tried to loosen the Beretta from the waistband.

The killer spotted me. He pressed in, and my hand slid off the gun.

"Not a good idea," he said with a seething look.

"I'm not trying to get anyone else killed today. Let's figure this out like men," I said, knowing how badly I wanted to shoot this guy between the eyes.

"Put your hands over your head where I can see them. I don't want you tempted to do anything stupid." He looked down at the old man lying in a pool of blood.

I stood erect with my hands in the air, feeling the cold of the gun against my skin, not knowing what to do.

"Don't do anything you'd regret. My partner is right inside that barn and he already called the police."

The bearded man lifted the butt of the knife and came down on my temple. I felt my knees buckle.

Then black.

CHAPTER
TWENTY-SEVEN

MY EYES SLOWLY OPENED. I lacked the memory of where I was or what happened. A voice began to get louder and more focused. The grogginess lifted for a second and eyes cleared.

"Dexter. Dexter. Can you hear me?" John said, kneeling down next to me.

He sat me up. I rubbed my eyes and felt throbbing in my right temple.

"What happened? I heard a thump outside and came running over. You were on your face and the old man was bleeding out," John said in a panic.

I felt my right temple and looked at my hand to see blood in the palm. "I saw him," I said.

"Who?" John asked.

"The bearded killer. The guy we saw at Frank's and the man who ran out of the house when we found the woman. I know it was him."

"Are you sure?"

"I'm sure. I will never forget that beard and the grin. The grin makes me crawl. He hit me with a knife. Did you see anything?"

John pointed over to a group of trees next to the side of the house. "I didn't see him. But, I heard a car pull away by those trees."

I wiped the blood from my palm on my jeans. I stumbled to my feet, full of adrenaline.

A sickness surfaced in my stomach. I began to make a connection in my mind. "Do you think it's a coincidence we keep seeing murders? The last couple picks, in the middle of nowhere, we see the same guy slit his victims' necks."

John's eyes got wide. He scratched his brow-short hair. "You think Maria has something to do with this?" he asked.

"I don't know. But, she is the one finding the picks," I said.

My stomach hurt just with the idea of Maria being connected to the crimes. She was like family. "Let's not jump to conclusions. But we need to consider all possibilities."

"This isn't to be mean. Maria is not smart enough to pull off a murder ring. She's family, man. I don't want to go there. We have done a lot to help her out," I said.

John scratched his head. "True. But, it's hard for me to believe all of this is coincidence. Maria is top of my list for a suspect."

I stood to my feet with the help of John and looked at him with a half-smile. "Oh... no doubt. We live in a town that sees one murder a year and now three have happened right in front of our eyes in a couple weeks. There's a connection ... we just need to figure out what it is," I said.

We walked back to the van, feeling defeated, and I sat in the seat, the doors open. "I need to call the police," I said.

John knocked the phone out of my hand. "No way. We're all alone out here. The police are not going to believe we had nothing to do with this."

"Are you stupid? I saw the killer and we can give them a positive ID."

John paced outside the van. "If we are going to help Samantha catch this sicko, we don't want to be associated with these murders. It's better we vanish. Let's just leave like after the dead woman. Let the police handle the rest," he said.

I kept thinking about the new business and knew John was right. We needed to fly under the radar at all costs. Seeing the killer's eyes sent shock waves through my body. I imagined pulling out a gun and piercing him through the face with the cheers of a surrounding crowd of onlookers.

"You're right, John. Let's get out of here."

The van sped off down the gravel road, back onto the highway. I kept thinking about Maria and the possibility of her being part of the murders. *No way.*

I sat back in the passenger seat and grabbed my pounding head and began to doze off. I tried to make connections… Maria… killer… murders… Samantha… John… my eyes fluttered and slowly shut altogether.

Darkness.

CHAPTER
TWENTY-EIGHT

I BURST through the glass doors of Antique Adventures and watched Maria working on something at the computer behind the counter.

"So, weirdest thing happened today on our pick," I said with a smile.

"Did John get diarrhea again and clog a collector's toilet like last month?" Maria said.

I remembered the clogged toilet incident and almost lost my train of thought. "That was funny. But no, that's not what happened. We saw someone get killed. Again," I said.

"You're joking, right?" Maria shot back with a puzzled look on her face.

"Nope, serious as a heart attack," John said.

I walked around the counter, grabbed Maria by the hand, and stared into her brown eyes. "There's something we need to talk to you about."

I rallied everyone into my office and we sat at a round table.

"I don't want you to take this the wrong way. We love you like family," I said.

Maria peeked at John, and then back at me. "Of course, Mr. O'Kane. You've always taken good care of me," Maria said.

"This seems odd. The last three picks you sent us on … we've witnessed a murder. We saw a man have his throat slit as his wife watched. We found a dead woman in a bedroom near a pick. And, to top it all off, we just saw another man get stuck like a pig, and fall dead," I said, leaning back in my swivel chair.

Maria stared down at the round mahogany table. Her eyes began to well up in tears. "I'm sorry. I don't know what to say."

"What are you sorry about?" John asked, sitting on the edge of the table.

Maria sat up in her chair, trying to find the right words to say. "When I knew the money was gone. I got nervous. A man came into the shop looking for Dexter. He told me how to make some money," she said.

I shot up from the chair and paced around the office. "Who was this man?"

"I'm not sure. He had a gray beard, a little man."

I swiped a pile of papers resting on the table into the floor, "Do you know who this man is? He's a killer. I'm pretty sure he's trying to kill my girlfriend's family. And sounds like, maybe me."

"I know… He's been watching you. His plan is to pin all the murders on you and John. He will pay me a lot of money if he succeeds."

A small tear began to trail down the side of Maria's mascara-padded cheek.

I flung myself down on a chair and put my hands in the air and stared at the ceiling. I looked back at Maria. "You were going to pin a murder on me and John for a few bucks. All the things I have done for you, your family, and this is how you treat me?"

The floodgates of tears opened and Maria could barely speak. "I got desperate. I was not thinking. All I could think of was going back to the restaurant, my kids, and didn't know what to do."

"I didn't mean to put you in a tough spot. I will take responsibility for making you nervous. But, friends—family—don't kill each other for a few bucks. That's a bit extreme, don't you think?"

Maria slammed her head on the table. "I know. I am so stupid."

Samantha, I thought. I ran out of the room. I got on the phone and frantically dialed her number. Nothing.

I left a voice message, "Call me back ASAP. This is an emergency!"

I ran back into the room. I placed both arms on the table and put my face about six inches from Maria. "If Samantha gets hurt because of you, I'll never forgive you. I'm going over to her house to make sure she's all right."

"You want me to come with you, boss?" John asked.

"Yep, I am going to need backup," I said.

I jumped into the driver's seat in the van and threw a handgun at John.

"You might need this."

John looked at the gun like a foreign object. "I'm not sure, Dex. I don't know how to use this thing."

"Learn fast."

I pulled up to Samantha's house. A small ranch house, red door, and white picket fence. I noticed a black car parked in the driveway.

I called Samantha again to warn her.

No answer.

CHAPTER
TWENTY-NINE

THE STAIRS of her house were covered in mud and boot tracks. I pushed on the propped-open screen door and peered in. John breathed over my shoulder.

Samantha sat in the middle of the room, tied to a chair, a white piece of cloth jammed in her mouth, makeup running down her face.

A man stood behind and over her, knife resting against her neck. The steel glistened in the sunlight. "Hello, gentlemen. It's good to see you again. I knew you would come looking for your girlfriend, Dexter. That's what good boyfriends do," he said with a grin.

The man wore a black cap, brown hair poking out of the side —a bit younger than the bearded killer I expected to see.

"Let's make this quick, Dexter. You're going to turn yourself in and confess to the three murders. Or, your special friend gets an incision in the side of her neck. Like the others. Your call." He gently brushed the knife against Samantha's neck and she winced with every touch.

"Who are you? Where's the bearded killer? He couldn't do his own dirty work?" I asked.

"I'd be careful what you say. I'm the one holding the knife.

Let's just say I work in the family business. I'm helping Jack out." He smacked his gum.

"So, that's the killer's name. I didn't picture the bearded man as a Jack; maybe Larry, Quido, Bob. Why don't you get him down here and let him do his own dealings?" I said.

Samantha began to quiver; tears streamed down her cheek, onto the floor. The brown-haired man began to shift his feet. "No. That's not how this works. I'm the one with the knife and holding all the good cards. You need to fold, or this ends bad for you and all your little friends."

"How about this... Why don't you give Jack a call and we can talk in person. I am not really into the long-distance kind of relationships," I said, holding out my phone.

A purple vein protruded out of the side of the man's head. He shuffled his feet with my every comment.

He reached into his waistband and pulled out a gun with the other hand. "Let's think about what you're saying, cowboy."

"Cowboy? I'm no cowboy. I'm a picker. Do you know what a picker is?" I asked.

"You mean a junk collector?"

"Oh no. We collect antiques. Rusty gold. One man's junk, another man's treasure."

John shrugged in agreement and gave a small smile to the crazy man waving the gun.

"Enough chit chat, chief. Let's get back to the plan. You're going to turn yourself in. Take the phone in your hand and make the call. I will wait. Do it and no one else gets hurt."

"Wait a minute. You just called me chief. I thought I was a cowboy. I'm confused, am I a cowboy or a chief? Can you clarify for me?"

The man shuffled, looked around the room, and shook his head. "Let's review. I have the gun, you don't. Please stop with the talking; you're starting to give me a headache."

I gave a glance to John and then looked back at the gunman

and smiled. "You know what? I have a cure for headaches. My mother taught me a trick when I had migraines as a kid."

"That's sweet. But I don't care. Please make the call, or she gets a bullet in the head."

"Can I still tell you the trick my mother taught me for headaches? It's very useful," I asked.

The gunman dropped his hands in reservation.

"I should have a pill right here in my..."

I reached back into my pants and in one smooth movement, raised the gun, and fired a shot right between the gunman's eyes. His eyes froze open, blood spilled from the hole down the center of his face, and he crumpled behind Samantha in the chair.

"That's how you cure a headache."

John had leapt into the corner with the surprised gunfire. "What the hell, Dex? Are you crazy? You could have got her killed."

I walked over to Samantha, untied her arms, and removed the gag from her mouth. She gave me a hug. "You okay?" I asked.

"I want this to end. I need this to end," Samantha kept saying.

"You're safe. I'm here. We'll get him soon."

John walked over to the gunmen and looked down at the pool of blood. "Yeah, this could be a problem. We need to get rid of this *Jack* somehow. And I don't think you're going to get your house deposit back." He smiled at Samantha.

I stuck out my hand as if to say that everything would be fine. "I'll take care of it."

I replayed the shooting in my mind, scanning the room. It felt right.

CHAPTER
THIRTY

THE THREE OF us stood around the dead body on the floor, thinking about how to get it out of Samantha's house. John stood up with an idea. "I got it. Let's take it to my place and we melt him down."

I laughed. "Next idea, please. Melt him down? You have lost your marbles," I said.

John paced around the room, looking down at the dead body, examining it like a coroner. "I'm serious. In my lab, I've got chemicals that would melt this dude down in no time, no trace. We just need to get him out of here without anyone seeing us," John said, rubbing his hands together.

Samantha went into the kitchen to get a drink. I whispered to John, "You aren't serious? You want to melt this dude down like a candle with one of your crazy potions? That scares me."

John looked into the kitchen to make sure Samantha was not coming. "It will be easy. I have a large, fifty-gallon barrel. We throw him in, drop in some chemicals, let it simmer, and we're golden. But first, we need to figure out how to get this chump to the van," John said, kneeling by the body.

Samantha came back in the room with a box of trash bags.

"Wrap him up in the bags and we'll take him to the car when it gets dark. My neighborhood is quiet. No one will see us."

"I like your forward thinking. She's a keeper, Dex," John said, pulling bags out of a yellow box.

I yanked a bag from the box and rolled the body to the side, his arms hunched over like a puppet on strings. Samantha began wiping the floor with bleach. The puddle of blood in the middle of her living room had become thick and dry.

"I really don't think I'm going to get my deposit back," Samantha said.

John and I lifted the slumped-over dead body into a large trash bag. We wrapped the head, torso, and legs with the bags. The body now looked like a suit bag a business man would use for travel. Ready for transport to the van.

"It won't be dark for a while. Let's have a drink and wait it out," I said.

Samantha went to the door, locked the deadbolt, and scanned the neighborhood for suspicious people through the front window. "Looks clear. I'll get some beers."

CHAPTER
THIRTY-ONE

A COUPLE HOURS LATER, the sun down, John picked up the mummy body, and threw it in the back of the van. He stood at the curb and nodded to Samantha. I walked back to the porch.

I could see the weariness in Samantha's eyes, how she wanted all of this to end. "Everything is going to be fine. We'll take care of this. And, we'll find Jack. I promise," I said.

I gave Samantha a wet kiss and looked into her eyes. "Everything will be fine?" she asked.

"Promise."

A few minutes later, we arrived at John's brown 1970's ranch house. We pulled the van into the garage and unloaded the corpse.

John slid over to the right side of the garage and found a white fifty-gallon plastic barrel. He lifted it over his head, set it next to the body now lying on the cold garage floor, and uncapped the lid.

"This will be his new home. I need to make a batch of chemicals to melt him down. I've used this with small animals, never a grown man. It may take a minute," John said.

"You truly are a mad scientist," I said.

John's excitement at the prospect of melting down a human

being was disturbing. I knew he was hesitant to be part of the *new* business, but I could see a change in his face.

"I'm going down to the basement and will be right back," John said with a smile.

"I'll stay here and keep this guy company. I don't want him to get away," I said with a grin.

I sat on the steps leading to the house, reflected on the day, and put my head in my hands. The swirls of emotion filled my heart. I did not grasp what we were getting into. The enthusiasm of the *new business* adventure was exciting, yet fear swallowed me.

I sensed someone was following me; I turned my head, and watched a bird sitting on a tree. Thoughts of my family and a need to avenge their deaths didn't make sense, but felt needed.

John emerged, calling me into the garage. He held two glass containers filled with some kind of chemicals, and an extra hazmat suit. He threw the suit at my feet, opened the caps on the top, and began pouring them into the barrel. "Dex, I'm going to put a little of the chemicals in the bottom, throw him in, and pour more on top," John said. I nodded.

John wore a hazmat suit, and breathed heavy through a respirator, pouring the chemicals into the barrel. He pointed to another suit on the ground. "Hey buddy, put that on, or your face might melt off," John said, straining to breathe through the mask.

"Might have been good information before you started splashing that stuff all over the garage," I said.

"You're probably right. Kind of new to this," John said.

I put on my hazmat suit and watched John continue to pour the chemicals into the barrel. John then put the glass container on the ground and motioned for me.

"Time to put this guy in."

The tall, lanky man was hard to fit in the barrel, dead weight and all. We struggled getting his long legs and his bent torso all the way down in it. I pushed on his brown hair, forcing him further down in the barrel. His body was now contorted in a half sandwich.

John reached down and picked up a second glass container. "This is the good stuff. The first was for the base; this is the melting agent. When these chemicals react, they will begin to melt this guy down like butter in a microwave."

I nodded, pretending I knew what he was talking about. "So, I am a layman when it comes to melting down dead bodies. Will … like … everything get melted down—bone, the whole deal?"

"Yep. This guy will disappear. Like he never was born," John said.

John began to pour the red chemical on top of the contorted body. As the two chemicals hit one another, they began to bubble and fizz.

"Throw me the lid. We want him to marinate with the top on, in case this stuff bubbles over."

We stood over the bubbling body, smiling at one another. John gave me the thumbs up. Still breathing hard.

For a moment, in that garage, LeClaire felt safer to me.

A couple hours later, the body was soup. John and I picked up the barrel and dumped the invisible man, now liquid, in a creek that ran next to John's house.

It was as if he never existed.

CHAPTER
THIRTY-TWO

THE END TABLE of my bedroom was filled with beer cans and a marijuana pipe. I wasn't handling the newness of it all very well. An alarm buzzed in the background, and I searched the room, trying to awaken myself and figure out my surroundings. The pounding of my brain joined together with a memory of a melting body.

I sat in red boxer shorts, bare chested, tattoos covering my arms. I examined them.

The date of my wedding anniversary, son's birth, and eagle and anchor, the Navy symbol. I needed the reminders, the reminders of who I was, and what propels me into the future.

The cell phone on the table danced around with an incoming call. I grabbed the phone, cleared my throat, and tried to speak. "Hello? This is Dexter."

The tender voice of Samantha came on the line. "How'd it go last night? I never heard back from you."

I looked at the table of fun and smiled. "Oh, yeah, it went fine. Had a late night. It's all taken care of. John is one mad scientist. I will leave it at that. How was your night? You didn't stay alone, did you?"

"No, I spent the night with my mom and daughter. Everything was fine, but I couldn't sleep. I kept thinking about the man who came into my house. He almost killed me, Dex..."

"Did you know him?" I asked.

"I'm not 100% sure. I think he might be a distant cousin. If he's working with Jack, I assume he's related."

"How big is your family?"

"Biblical proportions. I can't keep track of all the aunts, uncles, and cousins. This makes all of this confusing."

"I'm confused, too. I want to know who else is involved in these murders. But, I hope this sends a message to Jack, and whoever he's working with."

"Me too. I need this to end soon."

I could hear the tenderness of Samantha's voice and the search of closure. We both needed it.

"I'm glad to hear you're safe and doing okay. I need to take a shower and get to work. I will figure out what our next steps will be. This is all pretty intense. Please lay low, and call me with any suspicious activity," I said.

"I am scared, Dex. I keep thinking about the man with the knife," Samantha said.

With a moment of hesitation, I said, "You want to stay at my place tonight? You can sleep on the couch, no funny business, I promise."

"I might take you up on that offer. I'll leave my daughter with my mom. I trust you, I think."

I turned off my phone and tried to shake the cobwebs out of my brain. My phone began to ring again in my hand. "Hey, Samantha, what's up?"

A man with a deep voice got on the line. "If only, Dexter. This is the man who's going to kill you. I see you are taking an interest in one of my family members. That's another strike against you. I don't like many of them right now," he said.

I gripped the phone as the muscles in my hands tensed,

almost crushing the plastic. "Is this Jack? I had a feeling you might be calling me after last night," I said.

Jack breathed exasperated breaths over the phone. "Yesterday did not go as planned. Mario proved his incompetence, like most of my family. But, don't worry, you will pay for this, and probably a few more from my family tree before it's all done. I won't be fooled again."

I stood up in my boxers and glided around the room. "Well, Jack, sounds like you have the next move. Let me tell you this. If you try and hurt me, Samantha, or anyone else in LeClaire, plan on reliving what Mario went though, only worse. And, it wasn't pretty." The words coming from my mouth were new. Fresh. There was a confidence in me, first time in a long time, maybe ever. I didn't fear Jack one bit.

"Dexter… Dexter. You have no idea what you've gotten yourself into. I've already killed my own family. What makes you think I wouldn't take delight in killing some of yours? Maybe a coworker? Someone like family? Do you know a Maria?"

I stopped pacing around the room and froze, blood seething. "Don't even think about hurting Maria. Leave her out of this. Revenge against your family is your own business; don't bring my family into this," I said.

"As you know, Maria is another failure. I had an easy way for her to make good money. Simple instructions. She failed, and now she must pay," Jack said.

I held the phone against my neck and bounced on one leg, trying to get jeans on. "Maria gets killed, you follow," I said putting my gun in the jeans.

"Oh, tough guy. Why don't you give Maria some last wishes, before I kill her?"

I paused to think about what he was saying. "No, that's not how this is going to go."

"Why don't you tell her yourself?"

Jack put Maria on the phone. "Dexter, I'm sorry for everything. Thank you for all you've done for me and my family."

I ran out of the house, jumped off the porch, and got into my truck.

I floored it to Antique Adventures.

CHAPTER
THIRTY-THREE

I LAID into the Ford F-150, speeding feverishly down the quiet highway to the shop. I reached into my flannel shirt pocket and pulled out a joint. The Zippo lighter had my initials engraved in the side, DLO, Dexter Lawrence O'Kane. Lawrence for my deceased grandfather.

I lit the cannabis.

I stared at the lighter and remembered the gift. John gave me the Zippo at my bachelor's party. The next day, the happiest of my life. I laughed, thinking I never smoked a day in my life when getting the gift. Now, it was a daily occurrence.

Blood pumped and boiled through my veins as I contemplated meeting Jack face-to-face. My hands shook as I thought about a strategy for a rookie assassin. *Do I walk in and shoot the guy? Do I try and talk him down? I don't know.*

I took a hit on the joint.

The parking lot of Antique Adventures was empty. I flicked the joint out the window, opened the door, and smashed it with my leather work boot. I reached into my pocket, pulled out mouth spray, and gave my clothes a shot for good measure. Habit.

The Beretta .92 was under my flannel shirt, cold against my

skin, and there was a small knife pressed against my boot. I hoped none of these weapons would be used today, for some reason.

I glided up to the glass double doors of Antique Adventures, peeked in with hands cupped around my face, looking for signs of life.

No movement.

I gently pressed on the door to engage a release. The shop was quiet, except for the humming of the fluorescent lights.

I slid up to the front counter and looked down, up, left, and right, as if to avoid setting off a land mine.

I called out, "Hello, Jack, you in here? Maria, anybody?"

A faint voice called out from the back of the warehouse, "We're in here."

I opened a metal door that led into the back storage ware-house of the shop—a large room with cement floors, high ceil-ings; it was sterile, and cold, the place where Maria processed all the antiques we found on picks.

The room was still.

"We're over here, Dexter."

A small older man with a gray beard sat on a metal chair, holding a gun across his chest. "Glad we could meet, old friend."

I was silent for a beat. "Where's Maria?"

Jack gave a low-level laugh and said in a hushed tone, "She's fine, for now. But I need something from you."

"Haven't you already taken enough? All these lives in LeClaire. Bloodshed ends tonight," I said.

"That's the price you pay when you're not loyal. When fami-lies are selfish, there are consequences. You remember our deal?"

I scanned the room and pretended not to be interested. "Refresh my memory."

"It's obvious I'm dealing with amateurs. You turn yourself into the police. Take blame for all the murders. Then, I won't hurt Maria, Samantha, or anyone else in this shitty community."

I glanced left to a large, black curtain used to sort and divide our picks. I stared one more second at the curtain. "Where's Maria? How do I know you haven't killed her yet?"

Jack leaned forward in a metal folding chair, and it squeaked. "You're right, Dexter. I might have killed her. Maybe you're not an amateur after all. Let me show you something."

He slowly stood, knees wobbling, and pulled on the black curtain. It slid across; I could feel the wind.

Maria was standing on a wooden chair, a noose of rope tied around her neck. Her mouth was stuffed with a handkerchief. The rope connected to a bar in the ceiling.

Maria mumbled.

I could not speak as I examined my friend shaking in fear. "Leave her alone," I cried out in anger.

Jack stuck out a palm with his phone sitting on top. "You're going to call the police right now, and turn yourself in. Or your Mexican friend breaks her neck and stops breathing."

"How do you know I didn't call the police? Tell them you were here?"

"Dexter… Dexter. I know you live in a small town of rednecks. But, you're a smart guy. I have already done enough damage. Any more is just icing on the cake," Jack said.

"I don't need to call the police. Your evidence is all over this town. Even your own family knows you're a killer."

"I'll deal with them later," Jack said.

I felt my body tense. The culmination of loss, death, and fear of losing everything I loved, for a second time, sent tremors through my nervous system. I slid a hand back behind my back and felt for my gun.

Maria made whimpering noises, her legs trembling in fatigue, as she stood upright on the chair.

"Let me repeat myself. Maybe you *are* a slow redneck that needs a reminder. You are going to take this phone, call the police, and turn yourself in. Your little friend will not get hurt, and I will sneak out the back door, never to be seen again."

I looked up at Maria, eyes wide with fear, knees now knocking.

"Well, you're holding all the good cards. I better do it." I grabbed the phone and began to dial.

John picked up the phone. "Yes, my name is Dexter O'Kane. I'd like to report a murder. No, I did not witness a murder ... I committed them. I want to turn myself in."

"Dex, what are you talking about?" John said on the other line.

"Please come to Antique Adventures off Highway 24. I'll be waiting. Thank you."

I handed the phone back to Jack.

"Wow, I'm shocked. I didn't think you'd do it. You are a loyal guy," Jack said with a smile. Jack looked down at the phone and noticed the previous number dialed. "No! You didn't call the police. Who did you call? That's not the deal. Who'd you call?"

Jack limped over to Maria's chair and kicked at the feet. Her entire body shot toward the ground. The only resistance, the rope around her neck.

Her feet hung two feet up from the cement. With her hands tied behind her back, legs swinging, she tried to get air in her lungs. The rope swung her side to side, and she twitched like a fish on dry land.

"Get her down. You can dial. I'll call the police," I screamed.

Jack pulled his gun on me, placed it between my eyes, with finger pulsating on the trigger. "New plan. I will find greater satisfaction in you watching your friend die."

CHAPTER
THIRTY-FOUR

I WATCHED HELPLESSLY as Maria's life began to expire.

"Here's how this will go. You're going to watch her die. I'm going to leave out the back door. This could've gone better for you, Dexter. You could have been loyal," Jack said.

"You don't need to do this. You've already won. We can still save her. Let her down." My eyes were blurred by tears.

"That's what happens when you are betrayed. Bad things. In this entitled culture, people need to know when they're wrong."

I stood still, hands pointed in the air, and Jack had the gun pressed against my chest. He looked at his watch. "I would love to stick around. But, I don't trust you, and have a feeling the police might show up soon. I am going to slip out the back door. She still might have a chance," Jack said.

"You won't come out alive. I promise," I said.

"That's nice. I'm leaving now. It's been real, Dexter. Don't try anything funny," Jack said.

Jack ran out of the back of the shop, where a car waited for him in the alley. They sped off, and I heard squeal of tires in the distance, then silence.

I leapt over to Maria. She was no longer making any movement. I tried to set her feet back on the chair, but the wooden legs were broken. I got under her, grabbed her flailing body, and pushed upward, trying to lessen the pressure on her neck.

I yelled, screamed, and cried for help.

I could feel her body losing life as it touched mine. I left her for a moment, and tried to find a ladder so I could use my knife to cut her down.

I dragged a ladder over to her limp body and pulled out my knife.

I reached up, grabbed the rope, and sawed ferociously, trying to release her from the noose. I sawed and sawed, and finally the rope snapped, and she fell to the ground on top of me.

Maria was motionless. Silent.

I leaned over her body and listened for a heartbeat.

Nothing.

"Maria. Maria. Please don't die on me. This is all my fault," I cried.

The back door to the warehouse swung open and John came running in. He stood next to Maria and me, huffing and puffing. "What the hell happened? I got your weird call and rushed over here. Did Maria hang herself?"

I didn't speak, sobbing. I wiped my eyes and tried to find words amidst the tears. "Jack did this."

"Jack? The bearded killer?"

"Yep. He set me up."

"Where'd he go?"

I pointed behind to the back door. "He ran out the back. I heard a car drive away."

John ran over to the back door, looked around the alley, hoping to find a clue. He ran back to me and Maria. "You want me to call the police?"

I sat in a pool of tears, the lifeless body of Maria in a heap next to my legs. "I don't want the police involved. We already look suspicious. We will handle this ourselves," I said.

"Come on, man. It looks like suicide. Maria needs to be treated right. What are you thinking?"

"I'm thinking we melt her down like our other friend."

John looked at me like I'd lost my mind. "She has kids. They need to know what happened," he said.

"I will deal with the kids. We can make something up. They are young."

I stared at John. Some kind of switch went off inside me. "This is the plan. This is the *new plan*, no questioning me."

John stepped back in reservation. "Okay, Dex. Whatever you think, but I'm not sure this is the best move."

"We need to get Maria out of here, and clean up the mess. I don't want anyone knowing what happened here today."

I went numb, pushed Maria to the side, and paced around the cold warehouse. I placed a hand on my head and continued to pace. "We're going to find and kill Jack. And, we're going to kill him soon. This is enough."

"What are we supposed to do? I think we're over our heads. This guy is sick, and we need to be done with the *new plan*."

I didn't listen to John. "This is the new business plan. Jack will die. You take care of Maria, and I need to do some stuff."

John looked down at Maria. "You're leaving this on me?"

"Figure it out. I need to call Samantha," I said.

CHAPTER
THIRTY-FIVE

I CALLED SAMANTHA, trying to erase the images of Maria from the recesses of my brain. My mind switched from her dead body to imagining Jack's dead body next to her, and a faint image of Lisa and Spencer being lowered into the ground.

I slammed a fist against the steering wheel.

"Samantha, this is Dexter. We need to talk. Where are you?"

Samantha was caught off guard by my pleas and fast talking. "I'm still at my mom's. Don't come here. O'Malley's?"

"I was thinking the same thing," I said.

"Let's meet up at seven, after my daughter is in bed. I don't want them to be alarmed," Samantha said.

"You got it," I said.

I hung up the phone and called John. "You good with taking care of Maria?" I asked him.

"I got Maria's body at my place. I'm going to … you know, do a meltdown. I'll make an anonymous call to Social Services, to make sure her kids are taken care of," John said.

"Thanks, John, for doing this. Make sure those kids are safe. I need to focus on finding Jack. We'll be in touch," I said, leaning the phone against my neck.

The guilt of Maria's death weighed heavy on my chest. I

didn't know whether to blame myself, Jack, or a combination of both. All I knew was that Jack would be mine, regardless of the cost. The murders stopped now.

I pulled my truck into an Army surplus store. I flung open the glass doors. The store was filled wall-to-wall with guns, ammo, knives, grenades, and other weapons. An overweight man behind the counter, wearing a black Navy tee shirt, greeted me.

"How can I help you, solider?" he said, with a small cigar poking out the side of his mouth.

"I'm just looking for now. But, I'm going to need some weapons and ammo," I said, looking up and down at the shelves of artillery.

"Son, you take your time. You've come to the right place if you need weapons. I can tell you what's hot, if you care," the man said, blowing cigar smoke.

"I need something not too heavy, but can fire off a lot of rounds if needed," I said.

"Okay. Sounds like you might be doing some hunting. I know what you need," he said, grabbing a brown-handled rifle off the wall and handing it to me. "Try this one on for size."

The weapon was a Remington 7mm-08. A small and compact rifle used mainly for deer hunting; I had decided a rifle would be less suspicious. I picked it up, and it felt comfortable in my hands.

I put up the gun to eye level and daydreamed about setting down Jack. *Bang. That feels nice.*

The man behind the counter stood back, folded his arms, and admired my technique. "You look like a guy who knows what he's doing. You a vet?"

"Kind of. I did a short stint with the Navy a lifetime ago."

He held out a fist for a bump, "A military brother. Good to meet you. I don't meet many young Navy guys in the shop very often. Mostly hunters trying to a shoot a buck. You a hunter?"

"You could say that," I said. I continued to scan the sea of weapons. "I will take the rifle and get a few more items. Load me up with a lot of ammo. What you got for knives?"

The man got a huge grin on his face and waved me down to the end of the long, glass counter. "Come down here and I'll show you what we got. Check this out," he said, opening the glass counter and handing a steel blade to me. "You ever see Rambo? This is his knife."

I held up the long, perforated knife, gazing with awe and wonder, and gripped it with my right hand. "That is a bad ass knife. You could take off someone's head in one cut, I bet."

He nodded. "With ease. Or, if you need to gut a deer, this will work wonders."

"Perfect. I might be doing some slicing and dicing soon. Deer, that is," I said, with a grin.

I turned around to examine racks full of army gear: pants, jackets, and the like. I pushed through the different sizes, picked one out, and held it up. I gazed at a black jacket with bulletproof material lined on the inside. I wrapped it around my torso. "How much for this one?" I asked.

"Fifty bucks," he said.

"I'll take it," I said, placing my wallet on the counter.

"When you going hunting? You know it's not deer season until November, right?"

I knew the man was becoming suspicious. "Pheasant. My buddy owns land, and wants to do a warm up run, before deer season. Thanks for your help," I said, racing back to the truck before he could ask more questions.

I drove to O'Malley's, made my way to the bar, and saw Samantha sitting at the counter sipping a glass of white wine. Her adult beverage of choice.

She stood up to greet me, and gave me a hug. A hug that lasted an extra few seconds. "Good to see you, stranger. You're running late. Everything okay?" she asked.

"I needed some groceries. I was going to eat dog food soon," I said.

I wasn't sure why I needed to lie. I felt comfortable in the new business; I felt comfortable with Samantha.

I ordered a Jack and Coke and began to share my plan.

CHAPTER
THIRTY-SIX

I STIRRED MY DRINK—JACK, easy on the Coke. I watched with fascination as Samantha touched her face. "I need to find Jack and I need your help. Do you know his last whereabouts?" I asked.

"He fell off the map over ten years ago. Rumblings he moved to Maine for a bit. Not sure who'd know where he is now," she said, sipping her wine.

"My guess, he lives on the outskirts of LeClaire. Every encounter with him was just outside town. I would not be surprised if he had a house in the woods. We live in a small town; options are limited. He can't snoop around too long before someone knows something," I said.

Something went off in Samantha's head. She reached down, grabbed her cell phone from a red leather purse, and scrolled through the numbers and addresses. "Aunt Nellie. She'd know Jack's last known address. That might be a start."

"How do you keep track of all these family members? Is everyone in LeClaire part of your family tree? Not good when half the town is being hunted down and killed, right?" I smiled and quickly frowned, realizing the inappropriate joke. "Ooh, sorry. Not funny."

Samantha punched me in the arm. "I'll call Aunt Nellie and find an address. Will that help?"

"Absolutely."

I was surprised as Samantha immediately gave her aunt a call, searching for the address. She nodded a couple times, said "okay," and "thank you." She scribbled an address on her napkin and slid it toward me. "Here you go, Dex," Samantha said, blushing.

"Dex? You've never called me that before," I said.

"I know. John uses it all the time. I thought it sounded cute," she said.

We locked eyes and didn't say a word; I couldn't speak. Didn't know how all this worked. It had been years since the awkward dating scene.

"I am pretty cute, aren't I?" I said, stirring my drink.

"Not when you think you are. That makes you ugly," Samantha said, finishing her wine.

"Samantha, I need to say something. I don't want you caught up in all of this junk. We are going to be okay, and I want you to be safe," I said.

"Thanks for your concern. I'm a big girl. I'll let you know when things go too far."

"*Too far.* How far are we now?"

"We'll have to see. But, I am using nicknames already, probably a good sign," she said, with a wink.

I ordered another drink, reached for Samantha's hand, and smiled. "These last few weeks have been crazy, but I would be lying if I didn't tell you that I think about you many times during the day. Let's not make this complicated and see where it goes," I said.

"Sounds good, Dex," Samantha said, with a grin.

Samantha's eyes fluttered and she stared down at the wooden bar top.

"What's on your mind?" I asked.

Samantha gripped my hand a little tighter and spoke softly. "Does the pain of losing people you love ever get easier?"

I stumbled over my words and answered back, "I'm not sure. I haven't lost many people close to me. But, people say time heals all wounds. That sounds like good advice."

I chaperoned Samantha out to the front of the bar and gave her a kiss. "When all of this is over. Can we talk about *us*? I know our relationship is complicated, but we need to talk about whatever this is," she said, pointing to me and herself.

"Sounds like a perfect idea. I'm going to Aunt Millie's to see what she knows. I'll snoop around, hopefully eat some of her cookies, and call you later," I said.

I fired up the truck, stared at the address, and felt Jack was within my reach.

CHAPTER
THIRTY-SEVEN

I DROVE the streets of LeClaire, looking at the addresses on the small, turn-of-the-century homes. I thought about the families in each of these homes. Representing people, hard-working people, just trying to get along in the world. Guys like Jack made a mess of it for everyone.

I peered through the truck windows, trying to find the house. I spotted the small, white house, slowed the truck to a crawl, and parked out front.

I jammed the Beretta in my waistband for safe measure.

I glided up the sloped driveway, scanned the quiet neighborhood, and watched leaves blow beneath my feet. A car drove by and the driver didn't seem interested.

It occurred to me, as I approached the house, that I didn't know exactly what I was doing. *What am I looking for? What do I ask?* I panicked, standing at the front porch.

I knocked anyway.

The brown door swung open and a tall, skinny, older man emerged. He flinched back, locking eyes on mine. "Hey, young man. You scared me. I didn't expect any visitors today," he said. The older man pulled out a corn pipe from his shirt pocket, lit it, and showed it to me. "You a pipe smoker? I got an extra if you want to join me for a few blows."

I tried to figure out who this could be—didn't seem like an Aunt Millie. But, the thought of a few hits on a pipe sounded good.

"Sure, old timer. I'd love to join you," I said.

The old man left the porch for a minute and reemerged with a pipe and handed it to me.

"This will do," he said.

He pulled out a plastic lunch bag of tobacco and packed it into his pipe. He handed me the bag. "So, what brings you to my house at this hour? What you selling? That's all who comes around these days," he said, taking a puff.

I laughed, put a pinch of tobacco in the pipe, and lit it with my Zippo. "No, not a salesman. I was in the neighborhood and knew someone who used to live in this house. I wanted to see what it looked like now and maybe meet one of the owners. It has some good memories."

The old man took a few puffs on his pipe and laughed at my explanation. "Who used to live here you knew?"

"I had an uncle who lived here a long time ago. I used to come over a lot on Sundays when I was a kid," I said.

He tried to relight his pipe and continued to listen intently. "That's strange, because I've lived in this house for over forty years, and the house is only sixty years old. You might be a little young to have an uncle who lived here. Are you sure this is the right house?" he asked.

I puffed my pipe and scratched my head, pretending to be confused. "I think so. My uncle died years ago. But this has to be the house, or I'm losing my mind. I remember reading books on this porch. The Hardy Boys was my favorite," I said, scanning the large wooden porch and swing.

"There's a loony bin on the other side of town. If you need to check in, I can drive you there. Because, there's no way this is your uncle's house," he said, as we shared smiles. "Tell me about this uncle; maybe I know him. Maybe he lived in the neighborhood."

"His name was Jack, and he grew up in LeClaire. He owned a used car dealership."

The old man ripped the pipe out of his mouth and slapped his knee in excitement. "I am not sure who you are kid, but somehow the planets have aligned. Jack is my name. I used to own a used car dealership."

I gulped and coughed out a plume of smoke. I set the pipe on a small table and looked the man up and down. "Are you messing with me, old man?"

"No way. I'm too old to be messing round anymore. My name is Jack Ford and I used to own Discount Cars off Highway 24 before the shop closed."

"Jack Ford. Used car dealer? That has to be the weirdest coincidence ever," I said, shaking my head.

The old man sat back on his rocker, puffed on the pipe, and smiled at our exchange.

"Let me ask another question. What happened to the dealership? Why did it close down?"

Jack got quiet, stared at his house slippers, and did not look me in the eye. He kept smoking his pipe and rocking in the chair. "I would rather not talk about it. It's in my past and doesn't matter anymore," he said, small tear running down his wrinkled cheek.

"Sorry for bringing it up," I said, staring into the empty street.

Jack's cheeks burned red. "You know what … I'll tell you. It was a long time ago, you don't know me, and I don't know you," he said.

"Don't worry about it. I'll just leave," I said, rising to my feet.

The old man held out a hand to stop me from leaving. "No, stay. It will be therapy for me," Jack said.

I lit up my pipe, looking forward to hearing the story.

"In my twenties, I opened a used car dealership in LeClaire. I had a dream of making this dealership the best on this side of the Mississippi. We started small, sold a few cars, and it grew into one of the best dealerships in the county. After years of success, I brought on a partner to take the business to the next level. He took over our operations and the business went even further." Jack paused, wiped his eyes, and continued the story. "When I got too old to run the business, my partner thought it would be a good idea to keep the business in the family."

Jack put more tobacco in his pipe and his face became sunken. "I tried to hand the business over to the family, and no one seemed to want it. I made tons of money in this business, and shared much of it with them. And none of them wanted it. I couldn't understand. We eventually closed it down."

"Family can be difficult. This is obviously hard on you," I said.

"Didn't mean to cry. I thought I was over this family stuff," he said.

"What happened to your business partner?" I asked.

"When my family didn't want the business, he moved away. We lost touch years ago."

"What happened to your family? You still in touch with them?" I asked.

He wiped another tear away from his cheek. "Not much anymore. After the business failed, I was very angry. I stopped talking to them. I didn't want anything to do with them. I didn't handle things well. Ten years ago, I moved away to live in Hawaii, kept this house. I didn't tell my family, and they don't even know I'm back in LeClaire. It's better this way. They probably think I'm dead."

I stood up and shook Jack's hand. "I need to pick up milk for my wife. Sorry to waste your time today. Good luck with everything," I said, handing back the pipe.

"Thanks for coming by today. This was good for my soul," Jack said.

I drove away and watched Jack wave in the rearview mirror. I needed Samantha to clear up what just happened.

CHAPTER
THIRTY-EIGHT

I DROVE through the streets of LeClaire, buzzing with excitement and a mixture of confusion with the new information on the *real* Jack.

Main Street empty like most evenings.

I called Samantha, giddy to share the new twist.

Come on… pick up.

The phone rang for ten seconds.

"Hello," Samantha said.

"You're not going to believe this. I went to the address you gave me for Aunt Millie. No Aunt Millie, only a guy named Jack," I said.

"Did you say Jack?" Samantha said. "Slow down. I can't understand what you're saying. You went to the house … and—"

"I went up to the house, not really sure what to say, and was greeted by an old man. We had pipes, smoked, and chatted a bit," I said.

"You smoked a pipe with a stranger?"

"Yeah, what's the big deal?"

"I don't know. Weird for a first visit."

"It's a guy thing. You wouldn't understand."

"So … someone else lives in the house. Aunt Millie is gone?" Samantha asked.

"No trace of Aunt Millie, just a man named Jack Ford. He told me how he owned a dealership, tried to give it to family, no one wanted it, and he became angry. A business partner gave one last gasp to the business with no avail. He moved to Hawaii and lost contact with all family. He's back in LeClaire, and lives in a house he's owned for forty years."

There were a few seconds of silence over the phone as Samantha tried to take all of my fast paced talking in and this new revelation. "Jack *Ford*, that's my maiden name. My contact for Aunt Millie must have been wrong. The name sounds kind of familiar. When your family is so large, it's easy to forget its members. This guy is either pulling our chain or he's the real deal. Where's the business partner?" Samantha asked.

"That is the question of all questions. He disappeared shortly after the dealership failed. Jack said, he lost contact with him years ago," I said.

"Then the killer we've been chasing around is not Jack. It's someone else. Someone who knows our family story and is trying to enact revenge from the past."

"The logical person for these crimes is the business partner. The man your uncle mentioned who left town never to be seen. Your uncle mentioned he was angry when no one bit on the family business. I didn't get a name … but he moved away and might be back for blood," I said.

"I vaguely remember an uncle who owned a used car dealership. And, there was a man who hung around and did most of his business dealings. I can't be certain; that was a long time ago. I bet someone in my family will know something," Samantha said.

"Of course you have family that will know something. They are endless, like air," I said with a grin.

"Funny. We need to track down info on this business partner. This might be the break we need," Samantha said. "I've been so angry with the thought of my uncle being a killer—the thought of leaving the family for all these years—and now it might be someone else. It's amazing how quick we can judge others," Samantha said.

"Your uncle seemed remorseful. I think time away in Hawaii was good for his soul. He knew what he did was wrong. He didn't handle the business and family in healthy ways. Maybe you can talk with him sometime. Hear his story."

"You're probably right, but I'm going to need time for this one. I will call some of my family and tell them the news."

"No way. Not yet. We need to stay focused on finding and stopping the bearded killer. I think pieces are coming together and don't want to complicate this with family involvement. Okay?"

"Okay," she said.

"But there is one thing you can do. You need to snoop around and casually ask some of your family who this business partner might be. Is there any more information we can find to nail this guy?" I asked.

"This will be tricky without alarming the family. We already have three people dead, no suspects, and who knows how many more this psycho might kill before it's done," Samantha said.

"Do what you can. I promise this will end soon and no more people will die," I said.

I drove down the road, thinking about the details of the case. I hated making these promises that deep down I didn't know I could keep.

One detail lodged in my mind. Whoever this bearded killer was, he was not working alone. I remembered someone driving the car the night Maria died.

The bearded man had help.

CHAPTER
THIRTY-NINE

I STOOD at the back of the warehouse at Antique Adventures, wiped my brow of sweat, and sighed. The sun was hot—abnormally so, for September.

The metal roof groaned under the oppressive heat.

I placed my hands on my hips and marveled at the building for a second. The symbol of years of picking and the ability to provide for my family with rusty gold. This warehouse was the largest in LeClaire.

I wandered around the back of the building, examining the ground. Patches of mud and dirt covered the cement ground. I tried to replay what happened on the day of Maria's death. The central picture of squealing tires and the killer running out the back door came to my mind.

I stopped in my tracks, knelt down, and examined a patch of mud-laden tire tracks. I touched it, wishing for a second that I knew what I was doing. The equivalent of staring at an engine block and having no clue of how to fix it.

In a sudden moment of inspiration, I remembered Willy.

Willy Hayes, the owner of Hayes Tire. He knew more about tires than any human should. I pulled out my phone. "Willy, this is Dexter, from Antique Adventures. I got a tire question. Would you be able to come by the shop for a couple minutes?"

"You bet, son. Anything rubber and tires, I'm your guy."

"Great. Come on by. I'll be at the back of the warehouse."

I waited for Willy to arrive, searched the alley behind the warehouse for clues, and wiped sweat from my head.

The more I searched, the more incompetence set in. I was a picker. I didn't know the first thing of assassin life. I knew how to find rusty gold, bid down a clueless collector, and run a business. Still, this new gig, although frightening, felt like a divine calling, something from above.

A blue, full-size Chevy pickup rumbled up next to me. Rust graced the undersides of the truck.

I snapped out of my mini-depression. "Hey, son, where you need me?" Willy said, arm resting on the side of the truck window. I pointed to the side of the building. Willy drove over, got out, and examined the tire tracks with me.

Willy bent down on his hands and knees to get a better look at the tracks. His eyes were apparently not strong, as he almost kissed the ground trying to decipher the tracks.

He touched the mud, not pressing too hard on the drying substance. He popped back onto his feet. "Well, son, I'm having a hard time determining the kind of tire. Best guess, looking at the tread, it's a winter style tire. The size, probably a large sedan, or small truck." He pointed to the track as he explained the difference to me. "You see this deep groove in the tire? These are winter tires, because you want the snow and water to get pushed out from the side of the tread. Keeps the car from hydroplaning or ending up in the ditch," Willy said, showing his missing bottom teeth.

I nodded my head, pretending to be interested. "Can you tell me anything else about the tire? Anything to determine type of vehicle?" I asked.

"Not that it's any of my business, but why do you care about these tracks?"

"Um… some kids have been breaking beer bottles behind the shop. I want to track them down and make them clean up the mess," I said.

"That seems like a lot of work for a couple of hoodlums messing around in your lot," Willy said.

I tried to divert attention away from the question. "It's important to me. This is my business and livelihood. I want my shop to be clean and presentable for the people of LeClaire. You know how it is, running a business. I don't want punk kids making our town a mess," I said.

"I see. Here's what I'll do for ya. I'll take a picture of the treads on my phone and try and get a match on the Internet. The police use tire matches to track down bad guys all the time. Or, if a person needs a particular tire that might be out of stock, we can track it down for the customer in the database. The Internet is pretty amazing," Willy said, with a wry smile.

"That would be great," I said with a smile. "I need this fast. Could you get me something today?" I asked.

Willy scratched his head and wiped sweat from his tan face. "You really want to catch these kids, don't you?"

"Really bad," I said.

"I'll do my best, but, it could take longer if they are old model tires," Willy said.

I shook Willy's hand and he left the shop. I continued to walk around the back of the shop, still curious if I could find more clues.

An unfiltered cigarette butt bumped up next to my boot. I picked it up.

I knew no one else in the shop smoked, other than the occasional joint, so I put it in my pocket. Maybe the driver of the car had been smoking and had thrown it out the window.

I didn't know how to track down a man who smoked a particular cigarette. With the anxiety of the killer being on the loose and not sure what to do next. I lit up a joint to forget my plight for a bit.

CHAPTER
FORTY

I LEANED against the leather seat in my truck, watching blurry objects pass before my eyes. Marijuana ran through my system, giving me a moment of calm. I decided to check in with John and see how he was doing. "Hey, big fella. How are things?"

John could hear the extra happiness in my voice. Best friends for life make it hard to get away with anything. "You been smoking again, hippie?"

"Maybe," I said, with a giggle. "I called to see how things went with Maria. Did you melt her?"

"Come on, man. She's a friend. Show a little respect. I'm going to blame the pot and let you off the hook on that one," John said.

"Sorry."

"Yes. I took care of it. Did you at least call Maria's mother to let her know she's missing? I don't want cops swarming around us until we get the killer," John asked.

I slammed my head against the steering wheel, almost causing my truck to run off the road. "Oh, shit. I totally forgot. I will call her later. I need this buzz to wear off. Are you doing anything tonight?"

"Cleaning my house of remnants of melted body parts. You, know, just another day in the life of a mad scientist," John said.

"You want to hang out and drink some beers tonight? I'm feeling a little lonely lately," I said.

"Wow, Mr. Anti-Social. It's been a while since you initiated bro time. I'd be honored to drink cheap beer with you, friend," John said, with a chuckle.

"I'll pick up the beers. Why don't you come by my house tonight about seven? You still drinking Miller Lite?"

"Of course. *Cheap, light beer in mass quantities*—still my motto. I need to keep my girlish figure," John said.

"You're an idiot. Miller it is," I said.

I shut down the truck, straightened my John Deere hat, and entered Quick Stop, looking for beer. I headed to the back of the store and was greeted by a wall of beer coffins. A customer was making small talk with the cashier.

My phone rang. "What else you need from the store, John? Cherry Coke?" I asked.

"I don't know what you're talking 'bout boy. This is Willy, from Hayes Tires," he said.

"Sorry, Willy. Thought you were my dumb friend. Any word on the tires?" I asked.

"Good news. Turns out, tires were purchased at a nearby shop. I can't give the name of the owner for confidentiality purposes. But, the tires belong to a late-model Camaro," he said.

"Perfect. That's all I need. Thanks for the help. Come by the shop, and I'll get you something nice," I said.

"I have my eye on some of your old cars. I'll come by soon," Willy said.

I hung up the phone, glanced through the front window of the store to the parking lot, and made a double take.

A black car sat parked at pump #2.

No way.

I walked back to the beer area and grabbed a case of Miller

Lites from the cooler. I glided toward the cashier in the front of the store.

A man wearing a pulled down baseball hat set Bourbon on the counter. I eavesdropped on the conversation. "You got any American Spirit cigarettes?" he asked.

The cashier reached above the counter to the cigarette storage. "I think so. Not many people buy the unfiltered kind these days," said the pimply-faced cashier.

I reached into my pocket and examined the cigarette from the shop at Antique Adventures. A headdress of an Indian was stamped on the side.

I glanced over the mystery man's shoulder as the cashier slid the cigarettes toward him. The symbol on the packaging matched my cigarette.

I eavesdropped on the conversation.

"Filtered cigarettes are for wimps," he said.

The cashier nodded. "We're all gonna die. Why not have fun before we kick the bucket?" he said, with a grin.

"I'm new to town. You know where I could stay for the night, a decent hotel? I stayed at a nasty Motel 6 last night. Found a cockroach in the sheets," he said.

The cashier got animated. "You want a nice place? There's a Holiday Inn Express, off Highway 70, about three miles from here. It's brand new, cable, free Wi-Fi, and they got one of those free breakfasts in the morning. Fanciest hotel in LeClaire," said the cashier.

The mystery man snickered. "Free breakfast, huh? Sounds nice. One more question."

"Shoot, traveling man."

"Do you know a Samantha Rose? I'm a distant cousin, trying to track her down, and surprise her. Does she still live around here?" he asked.

"Oh sure. She's Larry's kid, lives on Shelby Lane, last house on the corner. Sad story about her, all over the local news," said the cashier.

"What happened?"

"Three of her family members were killed in the last few weeks. And, her husband died a couple years ago. Pretty sad."

"Is that right? I'm sorry to hear that. Maybe my surprise visit will cheer her up?" he said, with a grin.

The mystery shopper turned to leave. I turned my head and knelt down, pretending to reach for potato chips. He looked my way, and turned back, focused on his bag of Bourbon.

I paid for the beers and talked up the pimply-faced cashier. "You ever seen that guy before?" I asked.

"He's come around the last couple days. Buys unfiltered American Spirit cigarettes. I don't sell many; makes him memorable. Said he's from out of town, visiting family," the cashier said.

I scanned the parking lot, eyeing gas pump #2. The mystery shopper pumped gas into the Camaro. Cigarette dangling from his lip. I pretended to not see him.

I got into my truck and continued to watch him in the rearview mirror. I waited for him to make a move. The Camaro fired up, took off down the highway, and I followed close, trying to get a better look.

I called Samantha. "Sam, this is Dex. Get out of your house now. Get to your mom's. Someone is coming for you," I said.

"I'm at work. What are you talking about?"

"I found the killer. I overhead a man, at the Quick Stop, asking for your address. He said he's a distant cousin."

"What? I don't know of any cousins who would want to see me. Most of my family lives here in LeClaire," she said.

"I'm following him right now. I think he's the killer. He bought cigarettes, the same brand I found at my shop. Don't go home," I said, adrenaline pumping through my body.

"You're going off a cigarette butt?" she asked.

"I matched the tires on the getaway car the night Maria died, too," I said.

"I'm impressed. I'll go to my mom's after work," she said.

"I'll keep you updated," I said.

"Dex, please, be safe."

"I'm not sure what that means anymore."

CHAPTER
FORTY-ONE

"JOHN, change of plans. I'm in pursuit of the killer. I overheard him say in a gas station that he was looking for Samantha. I need you to meet me for backup," I said.

John was caught off guard for a moment. "Are you high? Why should I believe you?"

"I'm sober, man. This is no joke. We might have our guy. I need backup. Meet me at the Holiday Inn Express on Highway 70. He might be headed there right now," I said.

"A hotel? Dex, I'm flattered. But, you know I'm not that kind of guy. You need to at least buy me a beer first," John said.

"Stop messing around. I heard he was looking for a hotel room and think he might go there first. Meet me there right now. And bring weapons and your deer poison."

"Okay. You're serious, aren't you?"

"Serious as a heart attack. If this is the guy, this ends tonight."

"Dex, be safe," John said.

"Yeah, I heard that already," I said.

I followed the mystery man, hanging back to not look suspicious. I reached behind me into the cab of my truck and yanked out a black duffel bag. I rummaged through the contents and threw my Beretta on the seat.

My deer hunting rifle laid slumped over against the passenger seat. I glanced at it.

Too big.

The Camaro pulled into the Holiday Inn. I parked in a spot across from the entrance and watched him go into the hotel lobby.

I waited for a few minutes, grabbed my gun, and shoved it into the back of my Levi's. I put on a John Deere trucker hat.

The automatic doors opened to the lobby and I pretended to not see the guy standing at the counter. He was talking to the hotel worker. "I'm from out of town. Need a place to land for the night. I only need one night."

"What brings you to LeClaire?"

"I'm here to visit family. It's kind of a surprise."

The young, blonde worker smiled. "That's so sweet. You must really love your family."

The normal conversation turned into flirting. "I would do anything for my family. You must like sweet guys?"

The girl began to blush. "Maybe."

"Maybe you should join me later in my room. You know what room I'm in," he said, with a smile.

"We'll see. Your room is on the third floor, 306."

"Thanks... I did not catch your name?"

"Rebecca."

"Thanks, Rebecca, hope to see you later."

I sat in the corner watching the whole thing go down.

What a dirtbag.

The man grabbed his rolling black suitcase and made his way to the elevators. I followed close behind, tipping my hat over my eyes. As the elevator doors opened, and were about to close, I snuck in with him.

"Almost didn't make it. Thanks for holding the door," I said, hitting number four on the elevator keypad.

"Hot one today," he said.

"Not normal for September in LeClaire. What brings you here, to this small town?"

"I'm just here for a couple days, seeing family. I don't get out here much."

I stared at the ceiling. "Yeah, I'm from here. Most people aren't coming; they're going."

"Why are you staying in LeClaire's finest hotel if you live here?" the man asked, with a puzzled look.

"Darnedest thing. Our house is getting tented for bugs. Got termites the size of rats. I've been living in this hotel for a few days," I said.

"That doesn't sound good," he said.

"No kidding. I've seen a termite wrestle one of my kids to the ground. My wife told me she's filing for divorce if I don't fix the bug problem," I said.

"Women. Your family here?"

"Probably at the pool or something. The kids love the pool," I said. "You got kids?"

"Never married. Bunch of nieces and nephews though."

"You know what, I never asked your name?"

"Name's Eric. Eric Lawson," he said.

I stuck out my hand. "My name is—"

Before I could finish my sentence, he said, "Dexter, Dexter O'Kane."

I stared into his eyes as they changed from wide to a squint. The man slammed his forearm against my neck. My back rammed against the metal wall of the elevator, and I heard the sound of flexing aluminum.

"This is how it will go. You're not going to say a word, and we're going to take a trip to my room," he said, breathing in my face.

I coughed, gasping for air, his forearm pressing harder on my Adam's apple.

The doors of the elevator opened as he spun me around. The light from a window in the hallway stung my eyes, and I felt a gun at my back. He looked both ways in the hallway to see if anyone was around. He pushed me down the hallway, pulled out his room key, and swiped the key pad.

A green light on the door lit up.

He pushed the door open with his free hand, the gun in my back, led me into the room.

He felt me up, looking for a weapon, and found the Beretta. "Did you plan to use this?" he said, throwing it on the bed.

"How do you know who I am?" I asked.

"Let's just say I've been watching you. You seem to be in all the wrong places these days," he said.

"Who are you working for?" I asked.

"Let's say it's a family business," he said.

The man pushed me into a seated position in a leather chair. He aimed the gun at my face and began to unbuckle his belt with a free hand.

"Sorry, man. I like women," I said, with a smirk.

He didn't respond.

He tied the leather belt around the chair and cinched it tight.

"That's good," he said. "Now we can chat."

"I don't chat with serial killers."

"How do you know I'm a serial killer? That's a bold statement, friend. We are not even acquainted yet," he said, pointing the pistol in my face.

"Are you planning to kill Samantha?"

The man laughed. "No, Dexter. I'm a distant cousin, here to surprise the family. It's just a family reunion," he said.

"You've done enough to this family already. You're not going to get away with this."

"You're assuming a lot, Dexter. I don't think you're in a position to make any audacious claims right now," he said.

There was a knock at the door.

CHAPTER
FORTY-TWO

A SECOND KNOCK on the door.

"Hey, this is Rebecca. I brought you your bag. You left it in the elevator. Is that offer still good?" she asked.

The man yelled back, frustrated, "I'm busy. Just leave it at the door; I'll get it later."

"We can't do that, sir. I will need to take it back to the desk. I need to make sure you get it—hotel policy," she said.

"Stay here, don't say a word, or you're a dead man," he said, opening the door a sliver.

"I'm sorry, honey, not feeling well. Must have been some bad Arby's," he said, looking over her shoulder.

The woman blinked, and tried to sweet talk him. "Come on. You can't spend a few minutes with me? You're probably tired from your travels. I can make you nice and relaxed. I just got off my shift," she said.

"Not interested, sweetheart," he said.

The man's eyes lifted above her to see a man standing behind her. The girl was pushed to the right, the door slammed wide open, and John tackled him to the floor. John, having a hundred-pound advantage, pinned him to the ground and threw his gun to the side.

John looked up at me. "You alright, man?"

"I'm fine. Those cheeseburgers finally came in handy," I said, with a wink.

The girl from the front desk threw the man's luggage on the floor. "Here's your stuff, jerk. I hope these guys mess you up good."

"Thanks for your help, sweetie," John said.

He flashed a twenty dollar bill, and she took it. "No problem."

The door slammed shut behind her.

"Why don't we get Dexter free, and you can take his place," John said.

John dragged the man across the green carpet and stepped on his neck while untying me. He tied the man up and began to question him.

"Looks like your plan didn't work all that well. This is where it ends for you. No more killing, and our town can get back to normal," I said.

"What makes you so sure I'm your guy? How do you know there's no one else working with me?"

"I've already met Jack. He told me everything. Sounds like you freaked out after the business failed. You're looking for revenge. That stops now," I said.

"Jack used to be a car salesman. You think he's telling the truth? I can't believe you fell for his mumbo-jumbo," he said.

John looked at me in confusion. "Well, if he's in on this, we'll fix him too," I said.

"How do you know he isn't killing someone right now? Maybe your new girlfriend, Samantha?" he said.

I leaned into the man sitting in the chair, the belt strapped around the waist. I placed my hand around his neck. "If Samantha gets hurt," he coughed out faint words.

"You're weak. Be careful of what you've gotten yourself into. This could end badly for you."

"I'm not worried about it," I said.

John pulled out a small, black leather case from his shirt pocket. He snapped on a set of heavy duty rubber gloves, opened the case on the desk, grabbed a syringe, and placed a vial of black liquid on the table. He shook the substance, tapped the glass, and opened the top.

He yanked on the plunger and watched it fill up.

I peeked at John to see what he was doing. "Deer poison?" I asked.

"You better believe it," John said.

John tapped down on the plunger. Black liquid dripped off the tip of the needle. He flicked it with his glove. "I think she's ready. You want to do the honors?" John said, handing me the syringe.

The man in the chair peeked up, and his grin turned to concern. "What do you mean deer poison? What are you going to do, freaks?" he said.

I stood over the man, looking down on him, syringe in hand. "There's something you need to know about us. While we might be assassins, we still have hearts. Killing can be done in humane ways—that's at least our philosophy. When I inject the poison into your system, there will be no pain. In a few minutes, as the poison flows into the blood stream, your organs will shut down one by one. Still pain-free, I promise. Once the heart stops, you'll meet your Maker. Hope things are right with the Big Guy Upstairs. You a religious man?" I said, examining the syringe.

Sweat beaded up on the man's face, eyes wide open. "Come on, guys. Let's think about this for a minute. We can work something out. I can make a quick call and end all the confusion," he said, knees wobbling.

"No, I'm tired of negotiating," I said.

I stabbed the syringe in the side of his neck, pressed on the plunger, and let black fluid flow into his jugular vein.

He screamed, and gave a last glance.

"I will see you in hell," he said.

John and I stood over him and waited.

After two minutes, his eyes slowly shut, and he slumped over in the chair.

John took off a glove, placed two fingers on the man's neck, and checked a wristwatch. "Two minutes. Personal best."

I looked over at John with a smile of a job well done. "What are we supposed to do with the body?"

"I already thought ahead. I brought special melting sauce, lye. It will melt the body and clean the tub at the same time. It's in the car," John said with a thumbs up.

"Glad you're on the team, big fella," I said.

We put the corpse in the bathtub and poured the lye all over him. A few hours later, it was as if he never existed.

CHAPTER
FORTY-THREE

I DROVE BACK to the shop, feeling a sense of relief for the first time in a long time. Not sure if the killer was working alone or not, I assumed the former, and felt good about our first business transaction in the *new* biz.

I had never actually killed a person, and the feeling was euphoric. I wasn't sure if this was a good thing, or if I needed counseling. I felt a reverberating happiness and confirmation that this was what I needed to be doing with my life, at least for now.

"I need to call Samantha and tell her the good news," I said to John, who was sitting in the passenger seat of my truck.

I picked up the phone and called Samantha. The phone rang a few times and went to voicemail. "Hey babe, it's me. I have good news. I think your problems are over. The killer is dead. I want to see you and celebrate. O'Malley's later? Call me," I said. I turned to John. "She's probably at work. I'll call her later."

"How you feeling about all of this? You know, the killing and all?" John asked.

I tossed my John Deere hat on the dashboard, brushed a hand through my hair, and smiled. "I couldn't believe how good it felt to stab that syringe in his neck and watch him die. It felt like justice, real justice, like this matters in the world. At least in our corner of it," I said.

"I know what you mean. The jury is still out about the death part, but the justice part felt good, real good. I hope LeClaire can get back to order. That's why we love this place, right?" John said.

I turned down the radio. "John, there's something I need to tell you."

"What's that? You thought my deer poison was amazing?" John asked.

"Yeah, it was, by the way. Good work," I said.

"You wanted to give me a raise?" John said.

"The money Samantha is going to pay us for this job—it's quite good money, and might get the shop out of debt. I didn't want to tell you, and please don't let her know I told you. I am not sure how I feel about it yet," I said.

John's eyes lit up. "Really? Is this going to make things weird for you guys?"

"I don't know. I like this woman, but don't even know what we are yet. I feel like I'm cheating on Lisa. I haven't been with anyone since high school. What do you think?"

"I'm no Dr. Drew, but sounds serious. You're not cheating on Lisa. You'll know when the time's right," John said.

"I was going to do the job even with low pay. But now, after the euphoria of the last kill, I'm starting to think about the future. What if we could make money doing this for a living? It's not about the money. But, the euphoria of justice is intoxicating" I said.

"What is this kind of work, anyway? Killers for hire?" John asked.

"Um, not sure. Maybe... justice fighters for hire. Assassins," I said.

John grinned. "Actually that does not sound all that bad. Pickers by day, and justice fighters by night. That has a nice ring to it."

John and I bumped fists.

"I actually feel happy for the first time in a long time. I never thought in a million years it would happen in this way. But, I feel like I've made amends with the universe," I said.

"I don't know about all of that, but let's enjoy this victory and not get ahead of ourselves. How do you get the word out on an assassination biz, anyhow?" John asked.

"People will find us, look at our resume. We melted down a few people and killed a serial killer. That has to count for something, right?" I said, laughing.

"This is not something you post on the Internet or in the phone book. Killers for hire: we'll send a bill after the kill," John said.

"Funny. Let's not kill the mojo. We'll keep dreaming," I said.

I called Samantha again, excited to share the news.

No answer.

Worry crept up in my throat.

CHAPTER
FORTY-FOUR

I SAT in front of a small TV screen, mindlessly flipping channels on the remote, and in my brain. My dog, Murphy, lay asleep in my lap. I scratched his ears. "Not a bad day, boy."

The movements of the day rolled through my head like an HD movie. The thrill of the kill was wrapped in peace, but it also felt right. The weariness of the day, combined with that of the last months, began to weigh on my eyes. The ring of a phone shot open my eyes.

Not recognizing the number, I gave a sigh, and picked it up. "This is Dexter."

A pleasant-sounding woman on the line answered, "Hello, Mr. O'Kane. My name is Mary and I'm from American Express. This is a courtesy call because we have not received payment per your agreement. We need a minimum payment in ten days or we will need to take legal action. Would you like to make arrangements for payment over the phone?" she asked.

I held the phone away from my face, stomach in a knot, and mouthed, *leave me alone*. "Yeah, about that. I'll get you something in a few days. I just worked a job, waiting for payment," I said.

"Would you like a reminder call in a couple days?"

"If my phone isn't disconnected. That's fine," I said, with a laugh.

"Thank you, Mr. O'Kane. I will call in a couple of days. Is there anything else I can help you with today?" she asked.

"Other than canceling my debt, I'm good," I said.

The lady hung up and my stomach went into nauseous mode, a feeling similar to when I heard my wife and son were killed in a car accident. The high of the kill was wearing thin. The reality of debt and a dead family was almost too much to bear. The darkness of the room stifled me. The light of the TV flickered in my face, the only light available in the moment.

I got up and returned from the bedroom with a small bag filled with coke. I opened the bag, dumped a small mound on the glass coffee table, and placed a dollar bill on the table. I rolled the bill into cylinder shape.

I carefully made small railroad tracks of cocaine and stuck the dollar bill in my nasal cavity. I breathed in a deep breath and snorted up the chalk like substance, and leaned back on the couch, wiping my nose with my hand. I sat legs spread wide against the couch, calmness filled my sagging body.

Tonight calls for the hard stuff. A little pick-me-up, I thought, peeking at Murphy sleeping on the floor. He continued to snore and rolled to the other side.

I crouched back down over the table and repeated my sniffing efforts.

I stared at the TV, not really watching the black-and-white movie, thinking. Thinking about the kill, debts, Samantha, Lisa, Spencer, the business. I called Samantha one more time.

She picked up.

"Finally, where have you been?" There was no answer. "Samantha, you there?"

The sounds of sniffling came though the line.

"Are you crying?" I asked.

"Someone else died today," she said, through sobs.

The room began to spin and the movie got louder despite the volume being turned down. "Who died?"

"My brother, Tom."

I began to pet Murphy and grip the phone tighter.

"I'm sorry, Sam. Can I see you? I have some good news."

"What's the news?"

"We got him today. The killer. I don't think he could have killed your brother. When did Tom die?"

Samantha sniffled. "This afternoon. The police said someone broke in and strangled him."

"Shit. How's that possible? I followed the killer around all afternoon," I said.

"I don't know, but Tom's dead. Are you sure you followed the right guy?"

I tried to recap the details of the day, the cocaine fog, making it difficult. "I ran into a guy at the liquor store. He said he was your cousin, and was looking for you. He wanted to surprise you," I said.

"What? I only have one cousin who lives outside Missouri. He doesn't even know me. I don't think that would be him," Samantha said.

"I figured he was lying, so I assumed he was connected to Jack somehow. The business partner looking for revenge. Maybe a lucky guess, I don't know. But he's dead."

"Should I congratulate you? This is all new for me. But, my brother is still dead," she said.

"Damn it. Maybe we did get the wrong guy," I said, flipping over the coffee table, coke dusting Murphy's brown fur coat.

I stood over the turned-over coffee table and coke explosion. It dawned on me that hanging with Samantha with a cocaine hangover probably was not a good idea for the sake of the relationship. "Sam, I think we should take a rain check on hanging out tonight. I'm going to bed soon. I had a long day and am wiped," I said.

"I need you right now," she said.

"I'll call you tomorrow. Let's do breakfast," I said.

"Okay, I guess, if you're busy," she said.

"Sam, I love you…"

I couldn't believe what I just said.

Silence on the line.

"Thank you, but I don't want to think about that right now. I like you and all, but this is too much for me right now. I liked things casual. Maybe we got involved too soon," she said.

"What are you saying? You don't want to see me anymore?"

"Maybe that's best, right now. I need to figure things out, and grieve with my family."

I hesitated and felt another tear build up in my eye. "If that's what you want."

"Give me a little space. I'll call you next week."

I threw the phone across the room.

I lay face down on the floor, took another line of coke, and fell asleep on the couch.

CHAPTER
FORTY-FIVE

I SIPPED ON MY COFFEE, black, as I drove to the shop. John was meeting me to head out for a pick. The prospect of getting paid by Samantha, added to a slowly hemorrhaging relationship, made me feel the need to make us some real money.

I slammed back an Advil, trying to ward off the solo party of cocaine and drinking the night before.

The memories of Maria greeted me every morning, handing me coffee, and usually yelling at me for not calling a potential customer, gone in the grave.

I could hear her laughter, loud and obvious. Her Spanish accent danced in my head. A tear dripped off my cheek and landed on the travel mug resting in my lap.

Shit. Maria's gone. I have to find our next pick.

The thought of extra work became a burden. The creditor calls, rocking relationship with Samantha, and killer on the loose made my stomach ache.

I burst through the glass doors and saw John sitting behind the counter, reading an iPad. "Did you realize we need to find our own picks today? That sucks," John said.

"Yeah, it just hit me on the way over. We need to hire someone, but they need to work for free," I said.

"You think Samantha would be up for it? Help us out for a bit, until we make some more cash?" John asked.

I turned my head, avoiding the question.

"Oh no. You got girl problems?"

"She wants to take a break. I might have been insensitive to her last night. Things are complicated with us, anyhow," I said.

"Does this mean we aren't getting paid?"

"Not until we get the *right* killer."

"How do we know the dude at the hotel is not the right guy? What if he is?" John asked.

"Samantha's brother got murdered yesterday. She thinks there's someone else connected to Jack. He died close to when we got our guy," I said.

"No way. Dang, that family has gone through the ringer. You think there's another killer working with Jack?" John swiped his iPad.

I sat in my black swivel chair and turned. "I don't know. I'm still having a hard time believing Jack is in on this. When I met him, he seemed genuine and remorseful. Why would an old guy like Jack care about a family feud that happened years ago? But who else could be helping him?"

John came out from behind the counter. "We can think about this later. Right now, we need to make money. Early bird catches the worm. And I know just the place: garage sales."

The collector often underestimates the power of garage sales. People know they will not make much money at their junk sales, but what most people don't know is that an item that's been sitting in your attic for thirty years might be worth thousands. That is where we swoop in and make an offer. We once found a painting worth a few grand that a grandmother gave to her granddaughter when she died.

One man's junk, another man's treasure.

John grabbed the *LeClaire Gazette and* scoured the garage sale section. "Cool. It's Friday and people love to start their garage sales early. We might need to make a Saturday and Sunday run if today is a bust. Especially since Maria is not here to find us picks. I am going to miss her," John said.

We got in the van, I drove, and John looked for a first pick. "Find a good one," I told him. "I need to be cheered up." I gave John a fist bump.

"They won't even know what hit 'em," he said.

John scanned the paper and yelled out an address. It sounded like a familiar address, but I was not exactly sure why. The van found the street. John hung his head out the passenger window to identify the right house. He looked around and noticed a bunch of tables sitting on the front lawn.

He pointed. "There be gold in them hills."

I shook my head and ignored his comment. I scanned right and then left up the quiet street. The neighborhood had a familiarity to it. "Oh, shit. I was in this neighborhood a few days ago."

I read the address on a post in the front yard. I looked at John, wide-eyed. "This is Jack's house."

"What? Jack, Jack?" he asked.

"I'm sure. We smoked pipes on that same porch," I said.

I stopped in the middle of street and looked around, not sure whether to go in. "I don't know, man. Should we go in? We can find another sale," I said.

"Why not? He's not a threat. You said he's cool," John said.

I conceded and walked up to the front lawn to examine all the treasures. Jack was talking to a potential customer and caught a glimpse of me in the corner of his eye. "I'll be damned, son, if it ain't my new friend."

I raised a hand and gave a half smile. "How's it going, Jack? We saw your garage sale in the paper and wanted to see what kind of treasures you might have."

"Glad you came. I'm trying to get rid of some of my junk that's been sitting in the garage for years. I don't have many people to give my stuff to, so figured I could find a good home for it," Jack said, with a smile.

I pointed at John. "Jack, this is my friend John."

John was already immersed in the multiple tables and a lawn filled with collectibles.

"We run an antique shop over off Main. I am going to take a look around and see what you got," I said.

"Ooh. That sounds like interesting work. Please, look around. Hope you find something good."

The strategy for the garage sale is to get a lay of land first. Find the themes. Are they a young family selling baby clothes and toys? Are they an older couple selling antiques and family heirlooms? You need to know what you are looking for.

Most of the prices at garage sales are too high. The goal is to talk them down. Which is easy, because most people want to get rid of their junk, not haul it to the Goodwill.

I maneuvered my way between old golf clubs, bikes, vases, and people trying to find treasures. As I dodged an older man yelling for a price check, a picture caught my eye.

A large, wooden frame with hints of gold paint shone in the morning sun. It appeared to be a photograph of a large family. Twelve people stood in the picture, some old, some younger. It was a very nice picture, probably taken at a family reunion at some point.

The frame was what I wanted. It was made out of antique wood, which was probably worth a few hundred bucks.

I knelt down in the grass to get a better look. I pulled the frame toward me and felt its weight. It was quite heavy.

I leaned into the picture and noticed two people. These two people were familiar. I got even closer to see who they were.

The first, the killer from yesterday. The second, a man with a gray beard.

I stood up and put the picture under my arm.

CHAPTER
FORTY-SIX

"HEY, Jack, I really like this frame. How much you want for it?" I asked, holding up the wooden frame.

Jack's face turned sour. He picked up the frame and took a long look, admiring it like a fine piece of art. "This is a picture of my family and some close friends. Taken a few months before I left for Hawaii. These were hard times," Jack said.

"If you don't want to sell it, I understand."

"No way. I need to sell it. I need to put some of these memories behind me. I'll take $30 for it."

"That's a fair deal. I'll take it."

I held up the new treasure, knowing I could make a couple hundred off it, and gave a satisfying smile. "One more question. Who's this guy?" I asked, pointing to a man with a grey beard.

Jack sat back in his wooden rocking chair and folded his hands together. His blue eyes lit up with animation. "That's my brother Richard. He died in a boating accident right before I left for Hawaii. Never found his body," Jack said.

I tried to contain myself. The face felt like my own family. I knew this man was the murderer. *There's no way he could've died over ten years ago*, I thought to myself.

"He was a great man. He worked with me at the dealership

and was one of our best salesman. He would have taken over the business himself, if he wouldn't have died. He loved selling cars and was dang good at it," Jack said, wiping a tear with the back of his hand.

"They never found the body?" I asked.

Jack's eyes began to swell red. "No. He was out fishing on Lake Sonoma. His boat was hit by another boat, and he drowned. We had a funeral, no body."

"That's too bad. I didn't mean to open up past wounds."

"No problem. Sometimes memories are all we have in this life. Hope you enjoy the frame."

"You're right, some memories need not be forgotten," I said, thinking about Lisa and Spencer. I waved to John, who was still browsing for items, and said my goodbyes to Jack. "Hey, big fella, let's get out of here. We can find a few more garage sales on the other side of town, the rich side." I winked.

John's arms were filled with items. "No way, man. I'm still looking. We're going to make a killing," he said.

I leaned into his ear and whispered, "I think we found another clue. Meet me in the van ASAP."

John paid for his items, ran across the street, and dodged a car speeding by.

I held up the frame and pushed it in John's face. "Look at this picture. What do you see?" I asked.

"Is this one of those magic pictures where images appear if you stare long enough? I love those," John said, holding the frame.

"No, moron. Just look."

John scanned the picture and pushed his face closer in. "No way. That's our killer. The one from the hotel."

I tapped the glass. "Keep looking. You see anyone else that looks familiar?"

John examined each face one by one, he paused on one. "Who is this bearded guy? He looks familiar... Oh, shit, that's our guy. The bearded killer."

"Jack told me the bearded guy is his brother, Richard. And you're never going to believe this: he died ten years ago."

"If he died ten years ago, we're losing our minds. We both have seen this guy. He must be a ghost."

I punched him in the arm. "He's not a ghost, you fool. He's obviously not dead. If Richard's the guy, we have our lead," I said.

John pulled the van out into the street and looked over at Jack, and waved. I gave a small wave and then looked back at John. "It's time we find Jack's brother. This time, we will make sure he's really dead."

CHAPTER
FORTY-SEVEN

JOHN DROVE the van down Highway 24, making regular checks at the rearview mirror. A black car pressed in close behind. He looked over at me. "You think Samantha could help us track down Jack's brother?" John said.

I tapped on the glass, thinking, trying to find inspiration. "I don't know, man. Things aren't good with us. We might need to go it alone. We'll find him," I said.

The car driving close behind the van continued to push on us. John adjusted the mirror. "There's an idiot riding my tail. I'm going to pump my brakes and give him a scare," he said with a smile.

"That's the worst. If he's in such a hurry, let him pass by. The highway is wide open."

John held up his middle finger in the rear view and waved at the car.

I grinned. "You're a moron. Are you ready to fight this guy when we get off the highway?"

"Bring it on, sucker."

The car sped up, pulled up to the right of the van, and John turned his head to examine the driver. A black Camaro hovered close to the van window. I glanced down at the driver.

My eyes met his. The car jogged my memory. Black Camaro. "John, that's the getaway car. That's the motel guy car. Look who's driving it now."

John leaned over my lap to get a better look at the driver. He had a grey beard. The bearded man raised his hand and returned the favor of the right hand of fellowship.

I pulled out my gun from the glove box and checked the loaded chamber. "Get ready for a fight," I said.

The Camaro veered into our lane and slammed into the side of the van. John and I almost fell out of our seats from the impact.

"He wants to play hardball," John said.

John yanked his wheel, returning the favor, slamming into the side of the Camaro. The sound of grinding metal and glass exploded in our ears.

"Take that, son. Our van may be for picking, but it's bigger than yours," John said.

"Easy, big fella. This thing is not paid off yet," I said.

The driver of the Camaro pulled over to his lane one more time, ramming into my door. My head slammed against the passenger window. I grabbed it in pain, gun falling to the floor. "We need to stop this nonsense," I said, rubbing the side of my temple.

I raised my gun, stared down on the driver, and lined up my sight between his eyes.

POP. POP.

Gunshots blew out the right two tires on the van. The vehicle spun out of control on the highway. It veered left, dipped down into a ravine, and tipped over in a hole.

Smoke and dust engulfed the vehicle.

We lay sideways, still strapped into our seat belts. I was on the bottom, looking up at John. "You okay?"

John appeared to have no injuries. "I am okay. That bastard shot out my tires. How are you?"

I wiped my head, and looked at my hand. Blood covered my palm. "I have a cut on my head, but I'm fine."

A strange calm came over the overturned van. The silence broke at the sound of gravel being crushed by footsteps around the side of the van.

A voice emerged close to the vehicle. "Hello, Dexter," he said. "What a coincidence that we would meet like this. I've been watching you. I'm impressed by your abilities. It's a shame that you will have to die today. Such a waste of good talent."

I sat silent for a moment, gripping my gun, ready to fire. "I wouldn't be so sure of yourself. I think my skills are just starting to blossom. Don't get too close, or you might get a bullet in the mouth," I said.

"I'm sorry about your friend Maria. She was never supposed to die. But, that's the way this business goes sometimes. Appears you've been getting to know my brother," he said.

"Not sure how you landed in the same gene pool. He's a lot nicer than you."

The bearded man laughed. "He might seem nicer, but he's filled with hate and anger. He chooses to bottle it up like a coward. Now I am forced to do his fighting for the family. When family betrays you, they need to know they are wrong."

"Sounds like you need anger management counseling. Only true cowards blame others for their circumstances."

"What do you know about loyalty? Sounds like you weren't very loyal to Maria, not telling her about your failing business."

"Leave her out of this. You already got what you wanted. Careful about assumptions. They can burn you in the end."

The sound of splashing liquid began to slap against the tipped-over van. "I'm sorry it all has to end like this, Dexter. You got yourself mixed up with the wrong family. Family feuds are the worst." He laughed.

John looked over at me. "It smells like gas."

"I am leaving now. I have an appointment with your girlfriend. It might get a bit hot, but you're a tough kid. You'll be fine," the bearded man said.

"If you touch Samantha, you'll be sorry," I replied.

"Looks like you're not in a position to be making threats. Have a nice day."

He threw a match on the van and it ignited. Light flashed all around the van.

The heat instantly grew intense.

"I think I can get my belt loose, John, and then I'll help you get out," I said.

The sound of a car peeling rubber echoed in the van.

The van ached, as the temperature rose.

CHAPTER
FORTY-EIGHT

A GROUP of voices stirred outside the van. A man's voice yelled, "Is anyone in there?"

My arms dripped with sweat as the temperatures rose. "We're in here. Help!" I said.

I looked over at John, his large forehead covered in sweat. He was turning bright red. "Not a good situation for a fat guy. I'm sweating like a whore in church," he said.

I heard the sound of rushing water splashing against the bottom and sides of the van. A flint of water hit my face, giving me a moment of relief. One fireman sprayed the van with a hose and another stood above us, peering down inside the van as we sat suspended in the air.

"Can you move? Try unlocking your seatbelt," he said. I unlocked the seatbelt, climbed out of the shattered back window, and breathed in the clean air.

John sat patiently, still strapped in to his seat.

A firefighter climbed onto the top of the van and reached in to unleash John from his seat. John, not being the lightest man on earth, was helped out by two others.

"Thanks. It was getting hot in there. I thought we might be having John BBQ for dinner," John said with a grin.

I sat on the side of the ditch, looking at the charred van, smoke rising from the top, firefighters securing the area. My heart beat fast as I recovered from the rush of almost being burned alive.

A paramedic came over to give us oxygen through masks and tend our wounds. Nothing major, but we were taken to the local hospital for observation. I lay next to John on a gurney and was jostled as they put me in the ambulance.

"Just another John and Dexter adventure. Really bummed about the van. I think insurance will cover it," I said, giving John a wink.

A blonde paramedic leaned over me, checking my vitals. The intense moment of the van faded from memory and was quickly replaced with a picture of the bearded killer. A gnawing anger brewed in my gut when I thought about his face.

The image of his face, his laughing, and smug remarks as he set us on fire, made me want to leap out of the ambulance, and shoot him dead.

The paramedic looked at me, cross-eyed. "You okay?" she asked.

"Sorry. I remembered I left the coffee pot on," I said.

I stared at the top of the metal ceiling in the ambulance. The beeping of machines and the chatter of the dispatcher on the call radio faded in and out of my mind, and I shut my eyes.

Very quickly, I began to dream.

A small boy shot his dad with a water gun. The sprinklers were spinning as they laughed and ran through the yard. A woman sat on the porch, sipping iced tea, and smiled watching her boys play. The son threw the gun in the grass, walked up to the porch, and grabbed a couple sandwiches from the table and a glass of Ice Tea. Their faces went blurry.

I awoke.

A sense of happiness breathed inside of me.

I smiled.

"Dexter. Dexter. Time to take something for your pain," said a woman's voice.

A red-haired nurse stood over me. My eyes came back into focus. I scanned the inside of a hospital room and tried to get my bearings. She handed me a small cup of water and a pill.

"How long was I out?" I asked.

"A couple hours. We did a couple tests on you and everything looks good. You're a lucky man to only walk away with a few scratches," she said with a smile.

I panicked for a second. "Where's John? Is he alive?"

"John is right over here," she said, pulling back a curtain that separated us.

"How are you, big fella?" I asked.

"Good. A little smoke inhalation, but doing good otherwise. We're lucky, man," John said, sipping a large container of water.

I looked over to the nurse. "Could you give us some time alone?"

The nurse obliged and left the room. "If you need anything, let me know. Use your call button next to the bed," she said.

I leaned toward John; he was about five feet from me. "When we get out of here, it's go time. The bearded man is dead," I said, with unflinching eyes.

John laid his head on the pillow and stared at the sky. "I need to be honest. On the ride over here, I was doing some thinking. I don't know if I'm cut out for the assassin life. I sat in that burning van and wondered if I'm wasting my life. I want a wife, kids—you know, normal stuff. I want to be a picker, nothing more, nothing less," John said, avoiding eye contact.

I picked up a small apple juice from the side table and took a sip. "Are you shitting me right now? We've seen murders up close and personal. We've killed bad guys. We were inches away from taking out the bearded killer, and you want to give up. Don't give up now. We can get this guy."

"I think you're overestimating your abilities, Dex. You're no assassin. Finding the guy in the hotel was a lucky fluke. You know it. I think it's time we leave the *other* business aside, get our shop back in order, and forget all of this killing stuff."

"What if it wasn't a fluke? What if this is my destiny. What if we are called to something bigger in the world? What if we are more than pickers? John, you don't get it. This is not about us. This is about the people of LeClaire. This is about justice, and doing what's right. This is about taking down a killer who's destroying the lives of real people. Which includes someone I love very much, granted she's not talking to me right now. This is for the good of our city, our little slice of the world."

John leaned his head off the pillow to his right. "That was a nice speech, Dex, but I just don't think we're those guys. We're just a couple regular guys from a small town trying to make sense of it all."

My face began to burn red and feel hot. "Maybe I don't want to be a regular guy anymore. If you're not with me, I'll go it alone. I'd love to have you, but will not force it." I turned my head away.

"Please don't get yourself killed. I'm going to sit this one out."

I pulled the curtain back between us. I didn't want to look at him anymore.

CHAPTER
FORTY-NINE

I STARED at the phone like it was going to bite me. I paced around the room, eyeing it, butterflies in the stomach, stabbing a hand in the air, imagining an alligator snatching my finger. I needed to call.

I called.

Voicemail.

"Samantha, this is Dexter. I know things got weird between us. I want to talk with you. Also, I found an interesting clue about your family and want to ask you about it. Call me."

I opened a closet in the bedroom and pulled out a black duffel bag. I began to load in ammo, guns, knives, and an extra pair of clothes from the top shelf.

I set up a laptop and placed it on the kitchen table. I searched for "Black Camaro" on a website giving information on local vehicle registration.

I hit *enter* on the keyboard and thirty cars populated the screen. I sifted through the list based on area code and counties in Missouri. The search narrowed down to three cars in a fifty-mile radius.

My phone began to vibrate on the table. "Samantha? How are you?" I asked.

"I'm fine. Didn't I say 'next week'? I'm only calling you because of the questions you had about my family. What did you find?" she asked.

"I know you said next week. I'm sorry things got weird. I wanted to hear your voice. I want to work something out."

"We can talk about that later. My family? A clue?"

"I ended up at Jack's garage sale. John and I were on a pick, looking for antiques for the shop. The address we found in the paper was the same one you gave me a few days ago, Aunt Millie's, where Jack lives."

"I remember."

"Anyway, I was browsing his items and found a frame with a photograph of some friends and family. He told me the people in the picture were his business partner and his brother, who died. Richard."

"Richard? Richard was my great uncle. He died in a boating accident about ten years ago. I think it was right around the time Jack stopped visiting the family. He kind of disappeared."

"You're right. Jack left for Hawaii after Richard's death. The only problem is your great uncle tried to kill me and John yesterday. The dead uncle, not so dead."

There was a pause that felt like ten minutes. Samantha began to laugh on the other line. "Dexter, I know you're a smart guy, but you've officially lost your mind. There is no way Richard is still alive. I remember going to the funeral."

"I know you don't believe me, but the man I saw in that picture is the same man that is killing your family, and tried to kill me yesterday. I will swear on a Bible if need be."

"Tell me more about you almost dying?"

"Yesterday, John and I were coming home from our pick at the garage sale. This car tailed us and tried to run us off the road. He succeeded, the van got totaled, and he tried to burn us alive."

"Get out of here. Are you sure it was Richard?"

"Thanks for the sympathy. Did I mention we stayed the night in the hospital?"

Samantha giggled. "Yeah, that was rude. Sorry."

"Yes. I saw Richard before he ran us off the road. I assume he was watching us at Jack's house and followed us."

"I know I'm not supposed to like you right now, but I am sorry for you getting caught up in all of this. You really took one for the team yesterday. Thanks."

"Well, like I said before, I'm all in. I want this guy stopped. Do you remember the last place Richard lived? I don't know why I think he might still have a place here, just a hunch." I scanned the computer listing of Camaros.

"Why do you ask?"

"The car that tried to run us off the road yesterday was a black Camaro. It's the same car I saw another time when one of the murders happened. I wonder if we can trace his plates to an address."

"Did you say black Camaro?"

"Is that significant?"

"I have a black Camaro."

"What do you mean?"

"A few days before I met you in the bar, my car was stolen out of the driveway. It was a black Camaro. I never called the police, because a day later my family member was killed. I forgot about it. My aunt let me drive her Ford."

"You think Richard was trying to set you up by stealing your car?"

"I have no idea."

I looked back down at the website, touching the screen with my finger. "It appears your car is on page one of options. We find your car and we find Richard."

"Doesn't it seem odd Richard would use a stolen car? Wouldn't he be worried I would call the cops?"

"I don't know. I still think he tried to set you up." I paused. "Samantha, I want you to know, this job is *pro-bono*. I don't want your money. I'm going to find this guy."

"No. I said I will pay, and I will pay. I'm a woman of my word."

"I think the money is making things weird. It feels too much like *business*. Let's forget that part of it, and just let things be what they need to be."

"Sounds about right."

"I need to call the police."

CHAPTER
FIFTY

THE LIFE of a picker is often isolated, trolling the backroads of America. His human interaction is limited to toothless hoarders and imaginary conversations with cows in pastures. But once in a while, his work takes on a larger scope. It becomes greater than what meets the eye.

A church member looking for a certain Bible of their youth. The mother desiring to hand down an antique dollhouse to her newborn daughter. A police chief searching for a bike from his teenage years.

These are the items I find. They bring tears to the eyes. Especially the last one.

Two years ago, I did a favor for the local police chief, Jeff Riggins. I found him a Sting Ray bicycle from the 70's. He promised to help with anything I needed.

I needed that favor.

"Hello, my name is Dexter O'Kane, and I need to talk with Chief Riggins. He will know who I am."

A gravelly-voiced man picked up the phone. "This is Chief Riggins. How can I help you?'

"Chief Riggins, this is Dexter O'Kane. I'm a local business

owner, Antique Adventures. We worked with you a few years back," I said.

"Of course. You're the one that found my Sting Ray. I have it hanging in the garage. Can't wait to give it to my grandson when he's a bit older. How can I help you?" he said.

"This is awkward to ask."

"It's only awkward if you make it awkward."

"After I found the bike, you told me to not hesitate, to ask for anything, you were in my debt."

"I did say that. You finding that bike meant a lot to me, and my family. What you need?"

"A friend had her car stolen a few weeks ago. She never called the police, and I want to report it. But there's a catch."

"Okay…"

"I want to help you find the car. When you find the car, and the person who stole the car, I want to meet him, with you."

"Son, this is not how we do things at the police department. I can't let you get involved in a stolen car situation. If you want to do a ride-along that can be arranged through our office—"

"Chief, this is not a joke. I have information on the three killings that happened in the area. I need to be informed of when you find the car, and I will give you more information."

"Let's cut the bullshit. If you know of a possible suspect for these murders, you need to tell me. Now."

"I can't do that right now. This is personal."

"I don't care if this is personal. The law is the law. There is a *failure to report* law in Missouri. You don't want jail time, do you?"

"I have done most of the legwork to find the killer. You are going to help me finish the job. Imagine being the hero of LeClaire, when everyone finds out you took down this serial killer. This will be guaranteed seniority, and major resume booster."

The Chief waited a moment. "I am coming up for reelection in November. And, this would help the campaign…"

"If you crack this case you'll have a permanent job in LeClaire. You'll go down in public service lore as the *man*. Probably a museum in your name. Right on Main Street."

"I like the sound of that… Dexter, I'm a man of my word. I owe you a favor and that's what you'll get. This is a win-win for the both of us. Give me the license number, and your phone number. I'll get a detective on it right now."

I gave the Chief all the information and thanked him for the time.

"This means a lot to me, and this town," I said.

"Are you sure you're an antique dealer? You sound more like a detective to me. I'm looking forward to working with you, son," he said.

A smile spread across my face. "A crime-fighter doesn't sound bad to me."

"We'll be in touch."

The Chief hung up the phone.

CHAPTER
FIFTY-ONE

THE KITCHEN TABLE looked like a gun show at the Kansas City Convention Center. Guns, ammo, knives, and flak jackets staring back at me. I needed the call from the Chief to end all of the madness.

I sat down at the table and meditated on the image of the black Camaro. I wondered how the bearded man would die. What it would feel like. The conversation with the Chief played in my mind, and I grinned.

I called John.

"This is Dexter. I know you are scared. Hell, I'm scared. I don't know what we're doing. But I just had a chat with the Chief of Police, and he's helping us find Richard. He owed me a favor. Please call me," I said.

I opened the refrigerator and examined its emptiness. A couple beers, leftover Chinese, and expired milk stared back at me.

A joint would do. I deserved it after the conversation with the Chief.

I grabbed a joint from a small, black pouch in my shirt pocket. A kit for the weed smoker. Marijuana, papers, and lighter.

I opened the front door, fired up the doobie, rocked gently in my chair on the porch, and smoked my way to peace. Murphy crawled up next to my leg and did his usual sleep act.

John's truck pulled into the gravel drive.

A burst of dust shot up in the air. I threw my joint off the porch into the grass.

"What you doing?" John asked.

"Just contemplating the deeper things of life," I said.

"Ha. I got your message. Tell me about the Chief of Police," John said.

"Turns out Samantha's car was stolen a few weeks ago. A black Camaro. The same car Richard is driving around. I called the Chief, because he owed me a favor," I said.

"The '72 Sting Ray?"

"Yep. I reported the car, told him to call me when they find it, and we can go to work, I mean, *I* can go to work."

John shook his head. "The Chief went along with this?"

"Yep. He even told me that I'd make a good detective. Pretty cool, huh?"

"Have you thought this through? If they find the car, and let's say they do find Richard, what are you going to do? Shoot him on the spot?"

"Umm…" I paused. "I haven't thought that far. I figured once I find Richard, it will take care of itself."

"The other problem… now you have the police involved. We're supposed to be assassins. Law enforcement will not think highly of a couple vigilante killers. What if the Chief has a change of heart?"

"Why do you care anyway? Aren't you done with the *business*?"

"I do care. I care about justice in LeClaire. I care more about my best friend not getting his face blown off, or going to jail."

I stood up, and glided down the steps of the porch to meet John on the lawn. "Here's the deal. We—I—have nothing right now. My business is failing and on the brink of bankruptcy. Our vehicle, the thing that makes us money, up in flames. Our good friend Maria, dead. The girl I'm falling in love with is not sure about me anymore. My wife and son are in the ground. I do drugs and drink too much. I'm not a vision of wholeness and wellness. What do I have to lose?"

"Things aren't great right now, I get it. But, my life is not all that miserable. I'm okay, doing what I'm doing."

"Really? You live alone. You have not dated a woman since Clinton was in office. You spend your evenings doing experiments on mice in your basement. You have a lame Friday night poker game with high school buddies you barely like. You work for a failing business. And your friend was murdered. Need I go further?"

John gave a half smile and looked up at me. "When you put it that way, it does sound bad. A date would be nice."

"I need you, John. Your weird deer poison skills. And I need you by my side. We've always been partners in crime, all of our lives. Don't bail on me now."

John reached into his pocket and pulled out a glass vial. "I know I'm a loser. Probably need to spend less time in the basement lab, and more time with humans. But I think I perfected the deer poison. It will kill an adult three hundred pounds or less. In less than two minutes. Humanely, of course."

I held up the vial to the light. "See, I knew you're an assassin at heart."

"I don't know about that, but maybe this stuff will come in handy down the road."

I gave John a hug and whispered in his ear, "Thanks for caring about me, big fella. Brothers for life."

CHAPTER
FIFTY-TWO

MY BEER WAS GETTING warm as I discussed plans with John for taking down the bearded killer.

There was a knock on the door.

I got up to open the door and locked eyes on Samantha. She peeked around my shoulder and saw John. "I'm sorry for busting up dude time. I just wanted to talk. You guys have fun," she said, turning to walk down the steps.

I closed the door behind me and met her at the stairs. "Wait, Sam. I can talk."

Samantha stumbled over her words. "It's not a big deal. I just … wanted to tell you … I'm sorry. I feel like I put too much on you too quick. I should have never hired you," she said.

I grabbed Samantha around the arms. "I like you. I know family drama does not usually include murder. But when you date a woman, you date her family. It's a package deal."

"So we're dating now?"

"Call it what you want."

"Oh, yeah, I like you too."

"We cool?"

"We're cool." Samantha began to walk away, but she turned back. "Oh, I'm going to see Jack today. It would be good to reintroduce myself, knowing he's okay. I think it will be therapeutic."

"That's a good idea. Jack is a good guy and trying to put the past behind. Please don't mention Richard. That would kill him."

Samantha got into her car, sped off, and John came onto the porch. "Things okay with you guys?" he asked.

"Things are better. Sam is going to see Jack later today. Trying to mend the past, reintroduce herself."

"You think that's a good idea? I know he's probably harmless, but you never know in this town…"

"He's fine. He's an old man. I'll drive over there if need be. I know the address." I winked.

CHAPTER
FIFTY-THREE

"DEXTER O'KANE? THIS IS CHIEF RIGGINS."

I set my beer down on the outdoor table, wiped condensation from my hands, and tried to give the Chief my full attention.

John reclined in a lounge chair as the cool breezes washed over his face.

"Yes," I said with a cough. "How's it going, Chief?"

"We found the car," he said.

I looked at John, who was nodding off to sleep, and gave him a thumbs up. "That's great news."

"A neighbor called after hearing suspicious sounds at a house next door. The patrolmen found the car in the driveway. His orders were to call me first. He didn't make any arrests thus far; we are waiting on you."

"Did the patrolmen see anyone near the car or in the house?"

"He didn't do any snooping around. We don't know anything. Remember our agreement?"

"Of course. Give me the address and I will do my thing. Remember, Chief … this will make you look *real* good to the people of LeClaire. I see another term in your near future."

I scribbled down the address and hung up the phone. I glanced back down at the paper, scratched my head, and my hand began to tremble. "John, John, wake up. You remember the address of the garage sale? Jack's house. I forgot."

"429 Maple Street, or something."

I swiped my phone to check the latest addresses in my GPS. "Oh, shit. It's Jack's address. John, the car is at Jack's." I shook his arm.

John reached for his Cherry Coke, took a sip, and looked back at me, blurry-eyed. "What?" The information didn't register. "The car is at Jack's. That's not good. You think he's working with Richard?"

"I don't know. But Samantha is headed over to Jack's house right now." I dialed her number on my phone.

I ran into the house, pulled the Beretta from the shelf, and came back outside. "Looks like it's going down tonight. We're ending this right here and right now. You ready?"

John finished his Coke. "Let's do this." He gave me a fist bump.

"Sam, this is Dex," I began the message I left on her voicemail. "*Do not* go to Jack's house. Jack and Richard are there. They will kill you. Please call me back ASAP."

I revved the engine, jammed the gas pedal of the Ford F-150, and peeled out of the driveway. "If these guys hurt Samantha, I'm not sure what I will do," I said.

I weaved in and out of traffic, breaking speed limits, and garnering multiple honks. I called Samantha again, trying to not kill John in the process.

Voicemail.

John held up the vial of deer poison, flicked the glass, and watched the black liquid bubble up. "If we get in a pinch, this will come in handy. One touch on the skin, wait two minutes, nighty night," John said.

I pulled my Beretta from my waistband and placed it on the center console. "Hang onto the poison. But I think we're going old school. A couple bullets to the head, and call it a day," I said with a wink.

John nodded in agreement. "Be smart, Dex. We're not going to just walk up to the porch and start firing on Jack and Richard. We need to have a plan of action."

"Why not? If I have a clear shot, I'm laying them down."

"We need a better plan than this, Rambo. What if they're armed? Remember, we're dealing with a serial killer. And a dude with family anger issues."

I watched trees, cars, and people flash before my eyes, not focused on the driving task. "We kill anyone and everything that gets in our way."

John raised an eyebrow at me. "You okay? You got a weird look in your eyes."

The truck rumbled past Jack's house. I glanced out the window, scanning the driveway, and small house.

I slammed my hand on the steering wheel. "The Camaro is not here. John, the Camaro is not here."

"You sure? Maybe it's parked in the back, or around the corner—maybe Richard doesn't want anyone to know he's here."

I reached into the back cab and pulled out the deer rifle. I gave the gun to John. "You will need this. Watch my back. I'm going in the house."

I opened the truck door, checked both ways, and scanned the darkened streets. No signs of life in the house, lights off, no sounds coming from inside. I waved my hand for John to follow close behind.

I whispered, "I'm going to the back of the house to see if I see anything. You stand on the porch and shoot if they flee."

John played with the rifle, spinning it in his hands. "What am I supposed to do if they come out? They are not deer."

"Like I said, shoot them. Pretend they're deer if it helps," I said, with a grin.

I jogged up to the house, made a right toward the driveway, and disappeared to the back. John stood upright on the porch of the ranch-style house, trying to stay below the front plate glass window, which was not easy for his large frame.

I listened for sounds, squatting under a back kitchen window. Silence.

I reached up to a back door and wiggled the handle. I applied more pressure turned the handle. It gently yawned open, and moonlight shot through the house from the front.

I poked my head in, raised my gun to eye level, and scanned the kitchen.

"Now would be the time to make a sound. If you're in here, Richard, I promise, this will be the worst day of your life. Worse than losing the business," I said, gliding toward the front of the house.

No response.

"Jack, if you're in here, I hope you're getting acquainted with your dead brother. He's a piece of work. But you better not be helping him, or I'll need to kill you, too. I love LeClaire too much for you guys to be on the loose."

A creak of the floor awakened my heart. I spun around, swinging my gun.

Silence again.

I wiped a bead of sweat from my forehead with my free hand.

"Last chance to speak," I said.

Nothing.

I swung the front door and screen open. John aimed a shaky rifle at me. "Hey, big fella. They're not here," I said.

"Good Lord, Dex. I almost blew your head off," John replied.

"The way your hand was shaking, I wasn't worried," I said with a grin.

John followed me back into the house. We casually walked around the house for one last sweep. A handwritten note sat on the center of a coffee table.

I picked it up.

"Dear Dexter," I read it aloud, "if you're reading this letter, it's not a good day for you. Your special friend Samantha is probably dead by now. Nice try. Kind regards, Richard."

I collapsed to my knees on the floor, gun slamming to hardwood, and a tear ran down my face. I glanced up at John, whose head was hanging toward the ground.

"We're too late," I said. "We failed, big fella. Samantha is dead."

CHAPTER
FIFTY-FOUR

JOHN RIPPED the note from my hand, read it, and mouthed the words as he examined it closely. "Hold on. You didn't read far enough. There's a P.S at the bottom. It says Samantha lives if we meet him at Discount Cars, off Highway 24."

I ripped the letter back from John. "Let me see," I said, reading the letter again.

"Isn't Discount Cars closed down?"

"I think that's Jack's dealership. Doesn't matter, we're going." I threw the note on the floor.

"This sounds like a trap. You think we can trust this guy, after all this?"

"He's a psycho, yes. But, what else are we going to do? Samantha might still have a chance. That's a chance I'm willing to take."

"Should you call the Chief? Maybe he can back us up."

I stood up, wiped a tear, and checked my bullet chamber. "Nope. We're finishing this our way. Right now."

We marched out of the living room and back to the truck. John followed close behind. "You sure? A quick call to the Chief might be warranted," John said.

"Get your guns and poison ready. We'll need it," I answered.

We drove the dark, quiet streets of LeClaire. Streetlights glowed orange and the highway was sprinkled with cars.

I didn't say a word.

I gripped the wheel of the truck, replaying the blur of the last two weeks in my mind. I gripped the wheel tighter, almost ripping it from the dashboard. I looked at John, who was staring out the window. "Grab a flak jacket from the bag. I have an extra-large for you. Arm yourself with any weapons you might need." I shoved an extra pistol inside my jacket.

"Isn't this a bit much? We're not dealing with an army. It's a couple of old dudes."

"This old dude has killed a lot of people in this town. Be ready."

I didn't speak again until we arrived at Discount Cars.

CHAPTER
FIFTY-FIVE

THE CRACKED-ASPHALT parking lot of Discount Cars was overgrown with weeds, and a sign dangled from a pole at the front of the beige building. A sign spelling out *Discount Cars* sat high in the sky by the street, the red plastic with punched out holes.

John and I slid out of the truck, guns drawn, looking in the direction of the main office with a sign that read, CLOSED.

The breeze kicked up, and a small tumbleweed slapped against my boot. I looked up at a light pole, flickering with white light.

A voice came over the loudspeaker. "Dexter O'Kane. I see you got my note. Glad you could make it. You brought your fat sidekick too," he said, John shaking his head, staring at his belly fat hanging over his belt.

"Where's Samantha? I need to hear her voice," I yelled, voice echoing off the parking lot.

"I'm a man of my word, Dexter … unlike some people in my family. You read the note; Samantha is still alive."

A woman's voice came over the speaker. "Dexter … I'm okay. Please do what he asks," Samantha said.

"This is good advice. You see, when family don't listen to me, bad things happen to them," Richard said.

I spun around, trying to locate where the voices were coming from. "You're a coward, Richard. Only cowards hold grudges and punish the people they love. You need to get over yourself. No one else needs to die."

The voice got louder in the speaker. "*No*, Dexter! People who love you don't bail. They know when they have a good thing right in front of their faces. This dealership was built with my blood, sweat, and tears for forty years. It provided stability and wealth for this family. All they needed to do was sign the papers, and it might be thriving to this day. But, no... They backed out, and look what's left: nothing but this barren parking lot."

"I know you're hurt, but you need to move on. They have family therapists for this kind of stuff." I grinned.

"Therapists? You're a comedian now. Dexter, you have no idea the pain I've suffered. I have nothing left because of this backstabbing family."

"From what I can tell, you have a pretty great family. You sure you want it to end this way?"

"What do you know about family? You aren't even married, no kids. Is this a sore subject, Dexter?"

I bit down on my lip and clinched the trigger on the gun, almost firing a shot. "You don't know the last thing about me, or pain. Please tell me what you want, and let Samantha go."

The light posts lit up with a blinding white light. John and I shielded our eyes.

"Here's how this is going to go," the voice on the loud-speaker said. "You're going to call the Chief of Police and confess to the murders. Except you're going to actually do it this time."

My eyes filled with spots as the light beamed down. "Okay. No problem. Can you turn off the lights?"

The lights shut down, losing their luminous whiteness, and the orange glow returned. John looked at me. "You believe this guy?" he said. "We need to get a shot on him."

I nodded in agreement. "Let me see Samantha and you'll get what you want," I said to Richard.

The lights in the dealership showroom, about twenty yards ahead, lit up. We slid toward the building, surrounded in glass, on all four sides. I focused in on a convertible inside.

Samantha and Jack sat tied up inside a 1964 convertible Cadillac. Both of their arms were wrapped behind the leather seats and there were muzzles in their mouths.

I swung the door open, quickly cycled the room, gun aimed in every direction. John slid inside the showroom behind me. Gun aimed high.

"You like the car?" Richard asked. "I restored it for a special occasion like this one. The car, same year when I started working at Discount Cars."

"That seems like a lot of work for a coward," I said.

"Oh ... coward talk again. Cowards are people like my brother, here. People who disappear to Hawaii and let the business simply fade into oblivion. Who can't stand up for themselves and let their families dictate the course of their lives. If anyone's a coward, it's Jack."

Richard emerged from a back office, gun in hand, microphone in the other. He threw the microphone down. It screeched.

I aimed my gun between his eyes. "Leave Samantha alone. You know she had nothing to do with the business. She was too young."

"What do they call it? Accomplice to a murder... Samantha is an accomplice to the wrong family. Guilt by association."

Tears ran down Samantha's mascara-stained face. She struggled against the restraints and muffled sounds came from inside the Cadillac. We stood firm in the middle of the showroom, guns drawn, eyes still adjusting from the blinding light outside.

"You made a deal, Richard, right? I turn myself in ... no one gets hurt," I said.

"We have a deal," he replied, "but as you can see, if you chicken out on me, everyone dies. Get it?"

Richard slowly pulled back his jacket flap. His entire body was wrapped in explosives.

"No problem. You can watch me call the Chief," I said.

"Before you come any closer, I need you and your fat friend to drop the weapons, and put up your hands. They make me nervous," he said.

We dropped the weapons, put up our hands, and did what he asked. "Okay, Richard, we're following the rules. Let Samantha go, now," I said.

"I was not born yesterday, Dexter. Make the call, and I let them go."

I reached into my pocket. "I'm going to pull out my cell phone, is that okay?"

Richard reached into his back pocket and slid a cell phone across the black-and-white tile. "Use this one. All you need to do is hit the green button and you'll get the Chief, no funny business."

I picked up the phone, glanced at Samantha, and gave her a wink.

"Make the call, Dexter," Richard said.

CHAPTER
FIFTY-SIX

"WHEN YOU'RE DONE MAKING the call, slide the phone back to me on the ground. No funny business," Richard said.

I pretended to push the green button. I waited on the line for an answer. "Hello, yes, Chief, this is Dexter O'Kane. I have information about the LeClaire murders. Yes ... I want to turn myself in. I committed the crimes," I said. I held my hand over the mouthpiece. "Should I tell them this address, or somewhere else, to pick me up?"

"Don't tell them here. Give them your address."

I took my hand off the phone. "I'm at my home. 3770 Goldenrod Street. You can pick me up there." I hung up, and slid the phone back to Richard. "Done. Let these folks go. We had a deal."

Richard glanced down at the black cell phone and then looked back up at me. He held up the phone. "Wait a minute, Dexter. Looks like you never called, according to this phone. You wouldn't be lying to me, would you, Mr. O'Kane?"

"Come on, Richard. You didn't think things would be that easy. Why don't we settle this like men?"

Richard paced around the showroom, mumbling under his breath, "This was not a good move Dexter. You've seen what I can do. A rational person does not mess with someone strapped with explosives. This is not a good move…"

"You're not dealing with a rational person. What fun is that? I don't think you have the guts to blow us up. Your move."

"You know nothing about guts."

Richard raised his gun at Jack. He glided in and stood over the Cadillac. "This is my brother. He was a good man. But he's a coward. None of this would be happening if it weren't for his lack of backbone."

Richard pulled the trigger.

Brain matter splattered across the white leather of the Cadillac, and hit Samantha on the side of her cheek. She screamed.

"Now you know I'm serious. No more shenanigans, or your little Samantha is next."

I held up my hands. "Okay, Richard. I'm sorry, I shouldn't have lied to you. I will do whatever you want from here on out. Let's try this again. Give me the phone and I'll make the call," I said, waving to get the phone.

"I'm tired, Dexter. I'm tired of you, and all the drama. I got what I wanted. Jack is dead, and a few other disloyal family members. Samantha is just a pawn; you can keep her. Besides, I'm an old man, and I need my rest. It's been nice knowing you, Dexter. Hope everything works out."

"You're going to walk away, after all of this?"

"Yeah, I'm bored. I got what I needed."

Richard turned his back, walked toward a back door, and waved goodbye.

A bullet whizzed by my head.

John had opened fire.

A bloom of blood lifted in the air from Richard's right shoulder. He stumbled to the left, caught his balance, and jogged out the back door.

I slammed the front door of the showroom open, only to hear squealing tires, and catch the red glow of taillights.

I turned back to John. "Good shot, big fella. But what the hell were you thinking? You almost hit my ear."

"Sorry. I saw a shot and took it," John said.

"We need some time in the shooting range." I pointed at Samantha. "Get Samantha untied and take care of her. I'm going to follow Richard. You got the poison?"

John handed the poison to me. I placed the vial in my jacket, and ran through the parking lot, to the truck.

The black Camaro peeled out on the main highway in front of the dealership. My truck bounced out of the driveway and followed close behind.

I pressed the pedal into the floorboards, trying to keep up with the faster Camaro. We weaved in and out of sparse traffic, the city turning to country roads.

Richard made a quick right and the cement turned to gravel. The truck's shocks squeaked as the road pitched up and down over divots. I hit the windshield wipers and fluid, trying to fight off the dust and darkness. The pinging of pebbles ticked at the side of the truck.

Where the hell is this guy going? There's nothing out here.

The dust began to clear in the front of the truck. I scanned front, left, right, and back.

I panicked.

Richard was gone.

CHAPTER
FIFTY-SEVEN

I SQUINTED and hit the high beams on my steering column. The tires slid on the barren dirt road. I looked left and right, straining to see out of the windows.

No luck. No Richard.

The truck slowed as I looked for a turnabout to head back home. *He vanished.*

A cutout in a dark driveway that led up to a farmhouse. The first opportunity to turn. I veered right, spun the wheel, and waited for the truck to come back around.

I slammed the brakes.

A faint light blinked in my rearview mirror. I whipped the truck back around and headed back down the gravel road. In the distance, a small cottage with a single light hanging from the porch sat alone.

The muscles in my hands tightened as I got closer to the house. I slowed about one hundred yards from the house. I reached into my duffel, placed a small knife in my boot, released the safety on my Beretta, and put a second pistol in a holster under my jacket, because *you never know.*

I exited the truck, gun drawn. The only sound: crushed gravel under my boots. The only sound for miles.

I scanned the yard. A black car was parked next to a red barn on the left side of the small cottage.

My heart charged with energy.

A man emerged at the top of the porch. He was raising both hands in the air. I adjusted my eyes to get an accurate view.

"Welcome to my humble home, Dexter. I didn't think you'd keep up in that old truck. Why don't you come in and we can chat?" Richard said.

I smiled and stared at the ground. "That sounds like a trap to me. Where are your explosives?"

"I raised my hands for a reason. I want a truce. I'm tired and done with all the drama. The explosives ... weren't real, only for effect. I don't have any weapons or traps to pull, just a sore shoulder. Your fat friend landed a good one."

"Too bad it wasn't in the center of your heart. Maybe you'd feel the trail of pain you are leaving in this town."

"Dexter... Dexter. I know I've done some damage in this crap town. But I want you to come inside. There is something very important you need to see. It will be worth your time, I promise." Richard raised his hands to the sky.

I gripped my gun and moved toward him.

"I promise, no funny business. You need to see this."

I gradually climbed the wooden steps, creaking beneath my boots, gun raised, Richard sitting in an easy chair, feet reclined.

The small living space was lit with full light. I noticed the walls were covered in newspaper clippings, piles of paper on the coffee table, and photographs of people pinned on every free space.

I leaned in toward the left wall and kept my gun aimed at Richard. "Are these photos your family? The ones you killed?"

"Yep. I've been living off-the-grid for a couple years. Waiting for the perfect time. Looks like I'm the winner."

"Depends how you define victory."

I browsed more pictures. An older man with a hand drawn knife pointed at his neck. A beautiful, smiling, young woman with a red "x" scribbled across the frame caught my eye. "You're sick. Killing innocent people in this town. What makes you think I shouldn't kill you right now?"

Richard tapped a finger against an end table. "Depends how you define innocent. Besides, I'm a crazy old man. What would that solve?"

"Where do I begin? You have murdered four people—that we know of—and left a wake of misery for your family. That will solve quite a bit."

"What goes around comes around. But Dexter, I'm done now. That's the old Richard." He flipped the leg rests down on the recliner and glided to the far wall. "Come look at this article. You know these people?"

I gripped my gun, leaned against the wall, and read the article.

Mother and son die from a car accident.

I felt my eyes beginning to swell. "I know who they are. What's it to you? Why do you have this picture?"

Richard backed away about two feet. "I like to keep tabs on what's going on in LeClaire. There's usually not much happening in this sleepy town. When something like a serial killer on the loose, drought, or *car accidents* happen, things get exciting."

"Whatever gets you through the day."

"There's something else I need to tell you. I know this might be hard to swallow."

"Nothing surprises me anymore."

"What if the death of your family was not an accident? What if the car accident was a homicide?"

I paused, raised my gun again, and remembered the man in the black trench coat at the funeral. I laughed and examined the article. "That's not possible. The police investigation showed the car lost control after hitting a patch of ice. They died days later because of injuries sustained by the tree they plowed into," I said, trying to not choke up.

"Whatever gets you through the day," Richard said.

"Why are you saying their deaths were not an accident? What do you know?"

"I told you at the funeral."

I didn't answer.

"How do I say this? Your wife is related to me. A distant relative, but related nonetheless."

I moved closer to Richard and got in his face. "You have some nerve making the death of my family a joke. I should plant a bullet in your skull." I pressed the gun against his temple.

"Not a joke. Remember, the guy in the trench coat, at the funeral. That was me; I tried to make it obvious."

I clenched my jaw, no response.

"When I began my killing spree, Lisa and Spencer were the first. Except nobody knew it. I needed to prime the pump—a confidence booster if you will. A little monkeying around with her brakes, and the rest is history."

I paced the room, waving my gun, and holding my head. "What the hell are you saying? You rigged my car and killed my family to build your confidence?"

I lunged at Richard, grabbing him by the neck. I pinned him against the wall as newspaper clippings and other pictures floated to the floor. "Tell me why anything should stop me from choking you to death, you sick bastard."

Richard coughed and tried to speak. "Welcome to the family drama. You probably didn't think your wife set all this in motion."

Richard's compact body and legs dangled from the ground. The noises lessened and his face turned red.

CHAPTER
FIFTY-EIGHT

"I ACTUALLY THOUGHT for a second that I might have a change of heart. After seeing your house, not so much," I said, gripping Richard's neck with both hands, feeling the bones crush.

Richard's legs shook and dangled above the weathered wooden floor.

"I had another idea of how to kill you, but this will work," I said.

Richard's face turned red moving toward blue, and he tried to speak, saliva dripping from the corner of his mouth.

I felt a sharp pain in my groin. Richard's steel boot rammed between my legs.

I staggered, and loosened my grip on his neck. I dropped to a knee, and grabbed my nuts.

Richard lay next to me, rubbing his neck, and looked for my gun.

"I don't know if I'm done," he said. "Maybe one more kill."

Richard got up first. From the fetal position, I looked for my gun. He stood over me, pistol aimed between my eyes.

"You're a coward, Richard," I said. "You've taken life from

innocent people. It's a shame you'll have to die today. May God have mercy on your soul."

"Thank you for the sermon, but I'm not the church going type. Besides, it seems you might be meeting your Maker before I do." Richard engaged the trigger. He held the gun steady at my face and propped a cell phone against his cheek. "Yes, 911. This is Bill Young. I'd like to report a burglary at my home. The intruder is dead. Please send assistance." He winked.

He hung up the phone.

Richard placed both hands on the pistol and stared through me. "Sorry it had to end like this, Dexter. You seemed like a good family man," he said.

I lifted my shoulder, stared up at Richard, and gently swiped the glass vial from my shirt pocket. I covered the vial with my hand.

"Family is a weird thing," I said. "You never know how great they are until they're gone."

I reached back with the vial in hand and tossed it at Richard's face. The small glass vial shattered and the black liquid covered his wrinkled skin. I scooted back on my behind, avoiding the dripping liquid on his face.

He dropped the gun and staggered back.

"What the hell is this?" Richard said, wiping his eyes clear of the liquid. He staggered around the center of the room like a boxer about to go down for the count. A look of confusion set in on his eyes. He dropped to both knees, held his face with both hands, and then cupped both ears. "What did you do to me?"

I looked at my watch. "Right now, your organs are shutting down. The poison is making its way through the blood stream, and in about two minutes, or less … you will die. John ensured me it's a very humane way to die. We're not killers. We're just a couple of pickers."

Richard mouthed words, but no sound came out. He fell forward like a tree being cut down in the forest.

I rose up from the floor, massaged my groin, and walked to

the far wall. I ripped the article about my family from the plaster.

A tear trailed down my cheek.

I held the article down, kissed my index finger, and touched the news print.

"I did this for you guys."

I folded the article and placed it in my jean pocket.

Red and blue police cruiser lights blasted through the front window.

CHAPTER
FIFTY-NINE

I SHIELDED my eyes from the lights beaming into the small cottage. I found a couch to catch my breath. I glanced down at Richard's limp body, scanned the room, and gave a sigh of relief.

Did this really happen? I thought.

Two armed LeClaire police officers kicked the door open. "Freeze," they said, guns aimed at me on the couch.

"It's done. It's finished. He's the guy you want," I said, hands raised, motioning to Richard's body with a nod of my head.

A heavyset man with dark hair and a mustache came in behind the officers. "Dexter? Dexter O'Kane?" he asked, stretching out a large paw. "It's good to see you again. I'm Chief Riggins. Good work here today." He glanced down at Richard.

I stood up to greet him. "I'm just glad all of this is over. If it wasn't for the work of the LPD, none of us would sleep well tonight, knowing this killer was still loose," I said, giving a wink to the Chief.

"You're a hero, son. This will not go unnoticed."

"I'm no hero. Just right place at the right time."

The Chief scanned the room, looking at the newspaper articles and photos pasted on the walls. "This guy was a real psycho. Glad LeClaire can get back to some normalcy."

I pulled the Chief aside and said in a low voice, "I know this might be awkward, but my stomach is killing me. Could someone take me to the hospital?"

The Chief smiled. "I will take you myself. Right after we take you to the station for questioning. Standard procedure."

"Is there anything I should be worried about?"

"Not in this town. You're a hero, remember?" The Chief winked.

The Chief, the officers, paramedics, and crime scene investigators scoured the house, taking notes, pictures, and having conversation.

I stepped away from the voices to make a call.

"Sam, where you at? I have great news. Richard is dead. It's finished. Call me," I said, hanging up the phone, and shoving it in my pocket.

I glided to the front porch and stared out into the sea of cop cars, ambulances, and official vehicles. I took a deep breath of warm Missouri air.

Today was a good day. I could get used to this...

CHAPTER
SIXTY

I SAT ON THE PORCH, sipping an iced tea and washing down a pill for my stomach ulcer.

I watched a bird build a nest in a front tree while I waited for Samantha and John to show up. A smile bubbled up on my face, reflecting on the last couple weeks of life. I could have done without the nightmares of Richard taunting me with gun in my face, but all in all, things were working out better than expected.

I rocked back and forth in my rocking chair. The glass on the side table began to vibrate. The caller ID showed an 800 number.

I shrugged my shoulders, wondering who it could be, and picked up the phone.

"Hello, Mr. O'Kane, this is Denny from American Express. How are you today?" the man on the line asked.

I held the phone away from my face and mouthed, *shit.* "I'm great. How are the fine people at American Express today?"

Silence.

"I am fine … thanks for asking. We're following up about your payments that are past due. Would you like to pay that now over the phone, online, or mail a check?"

I rolled my eyes and covered the phone.

The moment you find a little bit of happiness, it gets squashed by the realities of life. Can't I get a break? I just saved our town, for heaven's sake.

"Yes, about payment…"

At that moment, a red car pulled up in front of the house. Samantha, John, and a little girl came running up to the porch, full of smiles and laughter.

I covered the phone. "I'll be done in a second."

"I'm going to need a couple days. I should have the money soon," I said to the creditor.

"Mr. O'Kane, we've tried to work with you, but, per our agreement, your payment is due now. If we do not receive something now, we're going to turn you over to a collection agency, or take legal action. How do you want to pay?"

Samantha handed me a white envelope.

"Open it," she said. "A little gift for you."

I leaned the phone against my cheek, opened the envelope, and nodded to the noise of the creditor. "I'm sorry, I don't have the money. I just finished a job, and when they pay, you'll get paid. I need a couple days."

I peeked inside the envelope and removed a check for $50,000.

"Mr. credit card man, can you hold one second?" I asked.

I set the phone on the side table.

"Samantha, I won't take this money. You need this for your family. The job was *pro-bono*. We already discussed this, right?" I said.

"Technically, yes," she answered, "but my husband left us a lot of money when he died. We'll be fine. Let's just call it a deposit on our relationship, and your new business. I don't plan on going anywhere anytime soon."

"Isn't this going to make things awkward… mixing business and pleasure?" I smiled.

"Only awkward if you make it awkward." Samantha bent down and gently gripped my hand. "This money is yours. You put your life on the line for me, my family, and LeClaire. That is worth more than money. You deserve it."

I shook my head. "I would've done it for free. But I'd be lying; the money is a nice bonus. I did almost die a couple of times. And, I know exactly how to spend it." I picked up the phone. "Denny, was it? I think my luck just changed. I'll send you the money over the phone in a few hours. Will that be okay?"

"That'll be fine, Mr. O'Kane. Please call to confirm you sent the money. Here is my direct number…"

I scribbled the number on my hand. "Thank you. Looks like I won the lottery after all." I winked at Samantha.

I stood to give Samantha a hug. Her daughter stared up at me with blue eyes. I knelt down to look at her.

"Hi, Lisa, my name is Dexter. I'm a friend of your mother's. How are you today?"

"I'm fine. How are you?"

I was taken back by her social skills. "I am doing a lot better because of your mommy. She's pretty cool."

"Yeah, I think she's pretty cool, too."

"You know what, Lisa? I need to tell you a secret, even your mommy doesn't know," I said, peeking at Samantha.

"I used to know a special person named Lisa. She was my wife. I also used to have a special person in my life, about your age, named Spencer. But, God decided he needed them in heaven. They passed away last year."

Samantha got a puzzled look on her face. "Okay. What is this?"

"About nine months ago I was married, and had a kid," I said. Samantha began to pull away from me. "Hold on. Hear me out."

Samantha yanked her hands away from me and put them on her hips. "Of course you did. Why didn't you tell me?"

I grabbed her hand again. "Let me explain. It's not what you think. I used to be married, and I used to have a son. But they died in a car accident. Actually, they were murdered."

Samantha slowly turned her head back to me, her face turning flush. "Are you serious? Murder?"

"My wife, Lisa"—I looked down at her daughter—"and my son Spencer were killed in a car accident. Turns out, someone messed with the brakes, and they crashed into a tree."

"Who would do such a thing?"

"Richard."

"Richard Ford, my relative, the serial killer?"

"That's the one."

"Why would he murder your family?"

"Lisa is related to him, and I guess, you too."

Samantha wrapped her arms around my neck. "Richard is a true psycho. I don't know what to say."

We both began to weep.

"I know every family is dysfunctional," Samantha said, "but mine takes the cake."

My tears slowed and I wiped my face. "Sorry for being such a baby. Not very tough for an assassin," I said through a forced smile.

John wrapped his large arms around both of us. "Okay, let's stop the touchy-feely stuff," he said. "How about we get pizza, beers, and play some poker? It's Friday night, and, Friday is for poker. Let's celebrate the victory."

I looked at John, turned toward Samantha, and bent down to Lisa. "You like pizza, Lisa?" I asked.

"Cheese is my favorite."

"Cheese it is." I gave John a hug. "Thanks for having my back. Partners in crime for life. Even though I think you're a loser who needs a girlfriend. Poker? Really?"

We all laughed and headed into the house.

The sun set and LeClaire felt a little safer tonight. At least for now.

A NOTE AT THE END

I wrote the first draft of this book in a contest called NaNoWriMo (National Novel Writing Month) in 2013. The challenge: write 50,000 words in 30 days or less, crazy right? I had never written a novel and thought, that sounds like fun, let's give it a try.

I finished the rough draft in exactly 30 days, hit save, and never looked at the manuscript until a year later. I am not sure why, maybe fear, maybe busyness, who knows?

But, I revisited the story in 2014, and began trimming, cutting, and molding something readable. In May of 2015, I sent it to an editor and she helped make it even better. Thanks Kari!

Why do I share this with you? To encourage, inspire, and maybe, kick you in the butt, if necessary. Maybe you're an aspiring writer with drawers full of manuscripts fearful to share with the world. A man/woman with a dream to start a business, non profit, or ministry.

I want to encourage you... do it!

This novel is not Hemingway, King, or Shakespeare. But, I did it. I wrote it. I finished it, edited it, bled over it, and now, I am sharing it. That's what it takes. Perfection is the enemy of fear. Stop allowing perfection to hold back your art, voice, or message for the world.

Second, I wrote this book for you. The satisfaction of writing this book only enhanced by readers, like yourself. My goal, someone other than my mom, would read the book, and maybe like it.

Maybe even tell their friends.

This is not a perfect book, no book is. But, sure was fun writing it, and hope you enjoyed reading it. Be gracious, it's my first novel, people.

Since 2012, I have written multiple nonfiction works, short stories, and completed two more novels. I'm getting better at the craft, and hope the stories will reach more people.

Third, I wrote the book I'd like to read. Every thriller and crime book these days are in big cities (NY, LA, London, etc.). I asked: What if a crazy psycho started killing people in a small town, where nothing ever happens? What if a normal guy became an assassin and saved the town?

I am a big city guy, and have always been fascinated with small towns and rural areas. I always wondered what life would be like growing up in these environments.

What I learned from talking with people from small towns is we all struggle with the same things. It just looks different in different places.

I also wanted to write a book that wasn't 600 pages long. I appreciate the Stephen King's, Lee Child's, and other main stream authors of the world. But, their books are bloated.

I want to give people 3-5 hours of page turning fun, and then move on. Maybe you like long books, maybe you don't. But, if you are like me, I don't have the time for this kind of commitment.

Nothing against the above authors (I love their books and read many of them). But, I wrote this book in a style for the average busy person who can plow through the book on the train, on the commute, or while the kid's are napping.

My style is my style…

Fourth, I am fascinated with families. Every family has a story, an interesting story. People who fought in war, worked interesting jobs, were psychotic, did ugly things, and did noble things.

Granted, in *Antique Assassins* these families are quite dysfunctional. Everyone has an uncle who wants to kill them (wink)?

Families are dysfunctional and we must embrace it. We must learn how to walk the line of grace and truth. I loved thinking about the dynamics of Jack and Richard. Dexter losing his own family. Maria, becoming like family, and losing her.

These themes were great therapy dealing with my own dysfunction and family dynamics.

This is probably not what you expected from an Author's Note. But, thanks for reading, hope you had a couple hours of fun, and check out Book 2: *Stranger Danger*. You will not believe what mess Dexter, John, and the Antique Adventure crew, find themselves in.

If you want free books before they are released and other cool stuff. Sign up for my newsletter at: ryanjpeltonbooks.com

Cheers,

Ryan J. Pelton

June 2015

NEXT BOOK IN THE DEXTER O'KANE SERIES

Available at all major book retailers (books2read.com/stranger-danger)

MEET DEXTER O'KANE

Thank you for reading Hired Gun.
I hope you had a few hours of enjoyment…

Dexter's adventures continue in a series of fast paced stories that take you into the underbelly of LeClaire, Missouri, and beyond.

The next story, *Stranger Danger*, finds Dexter reuniting with his father after a prison sentence. When a gambling debt hangs over the head of his absent father, Dexter and John, are forced to confront an Italian crime family.

Color Blind finds Dexter and John investigating a religious cult that comes to their sleepy town. When the leader of the cult is behind a slew of murders things get interesting in LeClaire.

First Blood, is a look into the origin story of Dexter O'Kane. How did Dexter become an antique collector and then a killer?

And *L.A. Dreams*, takes Dexter and John out to Los Angeles to help a local Private Investigator on a case. When the investigator is dirty, things get dark in a hurry.

The books are sold individually. But if you'd like to save a couple bucks, consider the *box set* for the first four books.

HELP ME REACH MORE READERS

ENJOY THIS BOOK? YOU CAN MAKE A BIG DIFFERENCE!

If you loved this book, you can help me reach more readers with a few easy steps:

(1) REVIEW THIS BOOK

Reviews are one of the best helps for getting these stories out to the world. My publisher doesn't have the financial muscle of New York, but does have an even more potent weapon. A bunch of loyal and committed readers. By leaving an honest review other readers can find and take chances on my books. Just go to the site you purchased this book, search for the title, and leave a review. Much thanks in advance!

(2) SUBSCRIBE TO MY EMAIL LIST

Building a relationship with my readers is the greatest joy of my writing life. I'm not just a writer, and love sharing things I'm learning, reading, and pondering. If you want an occasional update on the latest Dexter O'Kane novels, and my other writing projects. If you'd like to hear about things in my world, get some interesting links, and book updates please do so below. I also give special deals and other cool insider goodies to my VIP List. Sign up today, and join the fun! ryanjpeltonbooks.com.

(3) TELL YOUR FRIENDS

Word of mouth is still the best marketing there is, so I would love if you gave a shout out to your family and friends about this book, and the others I have written. You can find a comprehensive list of my fiction books at my publisher: attentionbooks.com

Thanks again for your help, and thanks for reading!

ABOUT THE AUTHOR

Ryan J. Pelton is a self diagnosed genre-nomad. His 23+ popular books span the literary landscape: mystery, thriller, crime fiction, middle grade, young adult, and spiritual nonfiction. Ryan is the host of The Art of Paying Attention, and founder of Attention Books. Ryan also is an ordained pastor, spiritual director, and coach.

When Ryan's not writing, he's probably reading, drinking too much coffee, and searching for the perfect taco. Find Ryan's latest books at ryanjpeltonbooks.com.